"You feel so good," Barry murmured in Megan's ear

He pulled her back farther into their hiding place behind the bushes, burying his face in the side of her neck.

"Oh, *Barry*," she moaned.

Hello? A moan? Already? He'd barely touched her. Still, he did have that effect on women.... "Did you miss me?"

"I feel so alive! I'm breaking rules...and I *like* it!" Megan shivered against him. "The adrenaline—my heart is pounding and all my nerves are hyper aware. This is what you feel, too, isn't it?"

"I get a zing, yeah."

She turned in his arms, which caused a zing of a different kind. "This is so much more than a zing! I feel hot. So, *so hot.*" She wrapped her arms around his neck and planted a quick, hard kiss on his open mouth as she ran her hands over his chest. "Why didn't you tell me it was like this?"

Barry was dealing with his own heat issues. "Who knew breaking the law would be such a turn-on?" he quipped.

And who could have guessed, Barry thought as he bent to kiss her, that the biggest turn-on would be breaking the law...*with a cop!*

Dear Reader,

I've always felt that a fail-proof way to test whether you want to spend the rest of your life with someone is to go on a long car trip together. Even better if you can borrow two children under the age of five to take with you. Inevitably, something will go wrong and that will be when you truly get to know the other person.

Under pressure, relationships can develop quickly in a short time—say 24 HOURS—which is the idea behind this new miniseries from Harlequin Temptation. And what's more stressful than a wedding? How about a wedding with a missing groom? Find out where he is, and join three couples who find love in a day beginning with *Falling for You* in March, followed by *Kiss & Run* by Barbara Daly in April, and Jane Sullivan's *One Night in Texas* in May.

Also watch for my next Harlequin Temptation novel, *Never Say Never*, in June 2005, and visit my Web site, www.HeatherMacAllister.com, for news about other upcoming books.

Best wishes,

Heather MacAllister

Books by Heather MacAllister

HEATHER MACALLISTER

FALLING FOR YOU

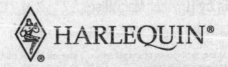

HARLEQUIN®

TORONTO • NEW YORK • LONDON
AMSTERDAM • PARIS • SYDNEY • HAMBURG
STOCKHOLM • ATHENS • TOKYO • MILAN • MADRID
PRAGUE • WARSAW • BUDAPEST • AUCKLAND

To the Providence Bunco group
with thanks for getting me out of the house

ISBN 0-373-69214-5

FALLING FOR YOU

Copyright © 2005 by Heather W. MacAllister.

This edition published by arrangement with Harlequin Books S.A.

® and TM are trademarks of the publisher. Trademarks indicated with ® are registered in the United States Patent and Trademark Office, the Canadian Trade Marks Office and in other countries.

www.eHarlequin.com

Printed in U.S.A.

1

FOR A GUY WHOSE PARENTS named him after the male lead in the seventies' sobfest *Love Story*, Barrett Sutton was not at all romantic. He could be if the situation called for it, but he had a talent for avoiding those kinds of situations.

Unfortunately, weddings were exactly those kinds of situations and Barry currently couldn't avoid them, not after being busted from crime reporter to the society section or "Lifestyle" section as the staff there liked to call it. Whatever they called it, it was now his job to report every little freaking detail about society weddings. And in Dallas, Texas, the society types had big, detail-filled weddings.

He hated it. Even worse, he was good at picking just which details to write about. Really good at it. And why not? He was a professional. A professional who'd grown up with sisters. However, if he didn't start misspelling some names or messing with the bridal-gown descriptions, he would never get back to reporting crime for the *Dallas Press*.

But this wedding wasn't the place to start misspelling anything. This wedding was the Shipley-Hargrove wedding. Yeah, the bride was party girl

Sarah, better known as Sally, Shipley—and try saying that three times fast. The society reporters had gone into mourning. Their favorite photo-op princess was settling down. Even worse, over the course of the year-long engagement, her posse of party-girl friends was settling down, too. Skirts were longer, tops were opaque, men were sober and parent-approved. Apparently this was round two for Miss Shipley, who'd actually been jilted before. Nobody was taking chances this time.

Barry hadn't been reporting society doings during the Sally heydays so there was considerable resentment when he'd drawn her wedding and the rehearsal assignment.

Yes, his life had sunk to this: professional jealousy over writing about lace, flowers and cake.

Hang the self-respect, he had to get his old job back before he lost all his contacts. It had taken him years to slide into a world where informants would trust him enough to talk. Now, instead of spending his nights buying rounds of the hard stuff in bars, he drank warm leftover champagne and tried to think up fresh ways to describe wedding cake and white dresses.

As he drove through Dallas, he gripped the steering wheel and allowed himself a moment of regret for the days of not so long ago, when a Saturday morning would find him finishing a story of murder and mayhem from the night before, and then heading home to sleep. Sure, some Friday wedding parties ran late, but stories about bacon-wrapped shrimp and "extravagantly massed nosegays of buff roses" didn't have the same urgency, even if he did file them while wearing a tux.

Tonight's Friday mayhem was nothing more than a bachelor party. But he *would* get back to reporting crime for the *Press* after this time-out in the penalty box. Usually reporters were honored for breaking a story. Barry's only problem was breaking it before the police did. He'd made a lucky guess involving a congressman, but the *Press* was making an example of him—an example that had gone on way too long, in Barry's opinion—but it was either suck it up, or quit.

The amount people spent on weddings was a crime in itself and in this case, the bride's family was loaded. The groom's, unknown. Barry could have some fun with that. He'd ask a few pointed questions and watch the spin over the groom's background.

Yeah, whatever. He pulled up in front of good old St. Andrew's. What was this, the twelfth wedding he'd been to here? And all in the daytime. From March until early June, the sun shone directly through the huge stained-glass windows. Apparently the architect had built it that way on purpose so that there could be some truly glorious Easter mornings. A number of brides chose daytime weddings to take advantage of the same effect.

Barry pulled into a parking place near the kitchen entrance. It made for a quick getaway if he needed one. Call it a holdover habit from his crime reporting days. Just because he'd been assigned to the society section—*Lifestyle* section—didn't mean he couldn't keep his skills sharp.

He turned off the ignition and swiped a stray pollen smear—pesky blooming trees—from the dash of his fully restored 1969 Ford Mustang Mach 1 351W. He needed wheels that blended in with the rich and famous. And since he couldn't afford rich, he went for famous, or in this case a classic car. It was a good excuse to buy something he wanted to buy anyway. Auto therapy. After last fall's public spanking, he'd needed a pick-me-up.

As Barry got out of his car, taking a moment to admire the blue finish gleaming in the midday light, a white Cadillac Escalade with custom peach, cream, and gold leather interior squealed into the parking spot next to his.

Paula Perry, wedding coordinator to the rich, exited the car.

He leaned over the top of his Mustang and made a show of checking his watch. "Rehearsal is scheduled for noon. Running late, are we?"

Her back to him, Paula dangled a pair of white satin pumps in the air. "Bride forgot her shoes. Can't practice walking down the aisle without these."

"Wouldn't retrieving them be the maid of honor's job?" he called, but Paula had already disappeared inside the church.

Barry slipped into the kitchen entrance just as a florist's van pulled in. It was silver with a calla lily tastefully framing a discreetly worded Whitfield Floral.

Ooh, boy. This could be good. Whitfield meant understated and just this side of stodgy. Barry grinned to himself. The bride was trying to leave her inelegant past behind.

Maybe, just maybe, he thought as he made his way through the kitchen, the bride and her bridesmaids were going to wear Vera Wang. He oughta send fan mail to Vera Wang. Nobody highlighted boobs as tastefully as she did. Sexy-elegant. His favorite look.

Still grinning, he headed for the sanctuary. If Paula verified Vera Wang, then he was bribing the custodian to turn up the air-conditioning. Cold women and silk charmeuse. Another favorite look.

Barry stepped in the side entrance and checked out the bridesmaids. They stood in a clutch, watching as the bride put on her shoes. They all wore the uniform of the sexy, young, urban single with the exception of one who had a kind of country-cousin look going.

Ah, the pity bridesmaid. The one asked as a favor to someone. She had potential, though. He wouldn't mind seeing her in a sexy bridesmaid's dress.

As he walked toward the back, Barry looked up to the balcony for the photographer and saw a man in black slacks, turtleneck and silver hair tied in a ponytail. Adolph Gunnerson in his I'm-really-a-serious-artiste getup. Barry let out a low whistle. The man, himself, was setting up tripods. He must think he had a good chance for pictures in *W* or *Town and Country*.

He waved. "Hey, Adolph." It never sounded right. Adolph wasn't a casual "hey" sort of name.

"Barrett."

Barry didn't even know how the man had found out his given name. He rarely used it.

Leaning forward, Adolph gripped the railing. "I

am the exclusive photographer and videographer for the Shipley wedding and associated events."

"Congratulations. I've heard they tip well."

Adolph glared down at him. "You will not need a press photographer. You will not need that." He pointed to the digital camera in Barry's pocket. "I will provide you with approved images for your paper."

"You know, Adolph, in this country we have a little thing called freedom of the press."

"Tell me again why you now report weddings?"

Adolph didn't like him. Barry tried not to take it personally because Adolph didn't like anybody. "Two o'clock deadline for the Sunday paper or we run with what I've shot."

Talk about surly. The guy probably needed carbs. In Barry's opinion, the world was a nicer place when people ate carbs. Carbs pillowed the hard edges.

He continued to the back where he could see activity in the narthex. The Whitfield florist and her assistants were assembling all sorts of white wrought-iron frames, ribbons, greenery and bows. The usual wedding glop. He pushed open the door. Might as well get the descriptions now.

"Barry Sutton, *Dallas Press*." He flashed an oversize press card he'd made himself. People always responded better after having ID shoved at them.

"What flowers will you be using for the Shipley wedding?" As he spoke, he smoothly pocketed his ID and removed a small tape recorder. Sometimes he took notes, sometimes he didn't. More often than not, he both recorded and took notes. There was a time when flowers wouldn't have merited either.

"Ms. Shipley has selected a white-on-white floral theme. She will carry bridal roses, gardenia, tulips, stephanotis, and our signature miniature calla lilies in a clutch bouquet."

"Very elegant." He was beginning to recognize the favorite combos florists used. This couldn't be good.

"We are always very elegant," the florist murmured in her smooth voice, as though they both didn't know that with enough money, the definition of elegant could be stretched tighter than spandex on a cheap hooker.

"Bridesmaids?"

"They'll carry three calla lilies."

"Class all the way." Barry clicked off the recorder and winked at her.

He saw a theme here. The bride was, indeed, distancing herself from her wilder days. Was this the groom's doing? Or had Mama and Papa—very nice folks; he'd met them—laid down the law? And if so, why now?

Which brought Barry back to the groom—who exactly was this guy? Ersatz royalty?

It was a mystery and Barry did love a mystery. He wanted to get his hands on a guest list. He knew there was one floating around. There always was at a wedding like this.

Usually, the security detail had a list to prevent crashers. Barry looked outside the church, saw the limos, but no large, serious-looking men with short necks and well-cut suits.

However, he did see Paula, the wedding coordinator, consulting with a slope-shouldered woman who looked both harried and important. A social secretary if he ever saw one.

Pasting on a third-degree smile—teeth showing with a hint of dimple—he approached her. "Hi there. You look like you're in charge. I'm Barry Sutton with the *Dallas Press*." He handed her a card. With some people, you got out the ID. With others, you gave them a business card.

"I know who you are." She took his card anyway. "I'll send you copy for your write-up."

As she turned back to Paula, Barry touched her on the arm. If a third-degree smile didn't work, physical contact usually did. "I write my own copy. I'm looking for a guest list."

"That's confidential."

"Hmm." Barry looked at her consideringly. "How can I put this…"

"Give him the guest list," Paula interrupted. "The more important the guests, the more column inches his editor will reserve. Unless you aren't interested in a premium write-up with mentions in the About Town and Fashion Sightings columns."

The secretary fingered the papers in one of her folders. "I…"

"What?" Barry spoke and heard Paula echo him.

"I'm not certain that is our mission."

What the— "I understand getting hitched is the 'mission.'" Barry used finger quotes. She deserved it. "Coming up with a story is my 'mission.' With a guest list, I can make a few calls ahead of time. Without it, I see who shows up and wing it." He took a step forward and lowered his voice. "By then, I'm close to my deadline. A little desperate for a good story. A little on the edge. Not discreet." He shrugged. "And who knows what my photographer might happen to catch on film."

The secretary paled and handed him a stapled packet of papers. "Here, but you must promise you won't bother the guests. Particularly—" She broke off. "Just don't bother them."

"I won't bother them. They all love me." Barry scanned the columns. Good grief. A cast of thousands.

"Here, Barry." Paula supplemented the list with one of her signature peach pieces of paper. "The official wedding schedule. Subject to change."

Barry studied the timeline. "Rehearsal begins promptly at noon." He looked at his watch, then made a note. "Guess it's going to be impromptly."

"We're waiting on the matron of honor." Paula gave him a tight-lipped smile. "She's pregnant and isn't feeling well at the moment." She glanced through the sanctuary door at the milling bridesmaids and sucked air through her teeth. "And it appears the best man is running behind schedule."

"No prob." Barry widened his smile to reassure her that he wouldn't write anything sarcastic because he knew Paula, and he liked her. She fed him information that was ninety-five percent correct, and she was fun after a couple of post-wedding martinis. Since she was married, he could flirt and she wouldn't take him seriously. Which was good, because he never meant his flirting to be taken seriously.

Barry slipped into one of the back pews and surveyed the scene at the front of the church. The bridesmaids, minus the country cousin who didn't seem to be there, all wore the urban style of short skirts and tiny belly shirts, along with the mother-of-pearl white high-heeled shoes they'd wear tomorrow. Very excellent fashion choices.

Barry allowed himself several moments to enjoy the sight, prayed for Vera Wang silk tomorrow, then scanned the guest list.

The names weren't in alphabetical order but were helpfully arranged by reception seating order. And in spite of what he'd told the secretary, Barry was very discreet. Otherwise, these people would never talk to him and he'd have to hang around parties to which he'd never be invited on his own. Which was exactly how he'd spent his childhood when he'd tagged along after his older sisters.

Most of the names on the seating chart were familiar to him. The Dallas old guard would be out in force tomorrow. Barry was struck by the number of the older generation who planned to attend. And then his attention was caught and held by one name— Donald Galloway. Congressman Donald Galloway.

Barry was instantly transported back to last fall and the investigation involving Representative Galloway. The same undercover investigation that Barry's report had exposed and that had landed him on wedding detail. He hadn't known Galloway was cooperating with the authorities. He hadn't known publishing the story would blow a two-year investigation. If someone had just *told* him—but Barry had found evidence of bribery and blackmail and figured he'd stumbled onto a scandal. And he had, but he'd ended up in the middle of it, along with Megan Esterbrook, the police media spokeswoman. He'd made lucky guesses in his article and she'd been accused of revealing too much information.

Barry had few regrets in his life, but getting Megan into trouble was one of them.

Megan. Earnest and sincere Megan Esterbrook. The Megan Esterbrook who could make a Girl Scout look slutty. The Megan Esterbrook who'd watched him when she'd thought he didn't know it. Who blushed, even as she grabbed for her gun. Potent combo, that. Barry stared off into the middle distance for an instant, then cleared his throat. He'd had thoughts about Megan—unprofessional thoughts he'd wanted to explore but the time never seemed to be right. And now she barely made eye contact with him.

Yeah, he felt bad about getting her into trouble, even though he'd just been doing his job. Megan was so heartfelt and so serious about everything while Barry had learned not to take anything seriously. Or not much, anyway. But her betrayed expression had stayed with him.

Right now, he was not going to think about Megan or her puppy-dog eyes. He was going to get back to business. Donald Galloway would be attending this wedding. Barry would not be chatting with him. Too bad, because he *knew* there was something behind the blackmail no matter what the official line was. Unfortunately, he had to play by the rules in order to reclaim his investigative-reporter status and the rules said hands off Galloway. Actually, the rules said Barry was to report society doings or never work in print journalism again. So that's what he was going to do.

Barry went through the list and starred the guests who he wanted to approach for comments and who he wanted the society photographer to shoot.

And speaking of pictures, Barry noticed that the bridesmaids were restless. Now would be a good time for him to take a few candid shots of his own. Though he wasn't the official photographer, the pictures helped him in writing up the gushy junk his editor wanted. Once he'd saved the day when the real photographer's equipment had been stolen along with all the wedding pictures. If one of his photos was actually used, it meant more money in his pocket.

He recognized Mrs. Shipley speaking to her daughter. Ah. A lovely candid mother-and-daughter moment. Daughter, wearing a more demure outfit than her bridesmaids—the skirt was Prada and maybe the top, too—and the mother conservatively attired in St. John Knits.

Barry held his breath, took the photo, then exhaled. He recognized fashion designers now. No real man should be able to do that.

Barry snapped more pictures—gotta love digital cameras—then looked around for the groom's family. Still none present, as far as Barry could see.

Paula and the secretary, both talking on cell phones, hurried down the center aisle. From the side entrance, the Whitfield florist began bringing in the now-assembled candelabra. Finally, some action.

Barry zoomed in on the face of the tough, serious-looking groom and a no-neck guy who looked like a bodyguard. Generally, the reactions of men as they're confronted with wedding excess were always good for a laugh and blackmail-quality photos. But the expression of this groom and the man standing next to him was lethally cold—and aimed right at Barry.

Something told Barry to keep taking pictures even as the two men turned away.

And then some*one* told him to stop.

"Sir."

The man without a neck thrust a hand over the lens. He'd moved fast for such a big guy. "You'll have to come with me, sir. We are not allowing photographs."

"Back off, fella, I'm the press."

Barry carefully set his camera out of reach and dug for his press card—the real one. He had a feeling this guy knew the difference.

Mr. No Neck studied the ID card, then grinned, revealing gold-framed front teeth. "Lifestyle? You mean parties and clothes and girlie stuff?" And Barry had to endure The Look, the one that questioned his manhood.

"It's a living." He accompanied this with a category-one smile—the bland, I'm-just-doing-my-job kind.

No Neck spoke into his watch, or something that resembled a watch, as he pressed his ear. In the meantime, Barry palmed a blank photo disk, just in case.

"You can stay, but no pictures and give me the disk." No Neck extended a hand the size of a catcher's mitt.

"Aw, come on. Give me a break. The paper didn't send a photographer with me."

No Neck gestured to the balcony. "He's the photographer."

Barry hesitated just long enough to make it believ-
able, fiddled with his camera and handed No Neck
the empty disk he'd palmed earlier.

"Thank you, sir." The man hulked down the aisle
and stationed himself near the side entrance, hands
in the classic fig-leaf stance.

Okay, this was getting interesting. That was more
than annoyance he'd seen on the groom's face. There
was a reason he didn't want to be photographed and
there was a reason the groom and this guy had taken
positions from which they could survey the entire
sanctuary while leaving their backs protected.

Barry's reporter's instinct kicked in. He wanted to
know those reasons.

While everyone milled around waiting for the missing matron of honor and cast anxious glances at the
double doors behind him, Barry got on the Internet
with his laptop to check out the groom's background.
He still had some active accounts at sites not publicly
available, thanks to connections he'd made and kept.

Smiling to himself, Barry clicked through the information he found. According to what he read, Augustus Hargrove, he of the threatening stare and
suspicious friend, had a background as pure as the
driven snow. Not so much as a parking ticket showed
up. Right. The guy had to have drifted somewhere.
Barry knew his type and his type always had an excess of testosterone that leaked out in a bar fight or
something similar.

The man was apparently a "security specialist"

for pity's sake. Everyone knew that was just code for ex-military or ex-secret agent. Really, once spies retired, what else could they do?

Hargrove Security Systems was a relatively new business, so what had Augustus Hargrove been up to before that?

The guy's background had been whitewashed. Very nice job. The problem was that it was too nice. It didn't fit a man who could look so threatening in a church.

Barry dug around some more. Any story he uncovered that was connected with this wedding was playing by the rules as far as he was concerned. The managing editor couldn't expect him to just ignore a hunch, could he?

How had Little Miss Party Girl hooked up with the guy?

Barry started in on Sally Shipley's movements for the past year, oblivious to when the wedding rehearsal began, coming up for air only when people passed him on their way out of the church.

Great. He'd pay for that later. But right now, he wanted to ask the groom some questions. So where was the groom? He hadn't been with the bride and her friends as they'd passed by. Barry packed up his laptop and strode toward the front of the church.

He was supposed to be concentrating on the bride, her bridesmaids and this afternoon's trip to the spa. Barry didn't want to miss the trip to the spa. That's where most of the society reporters went wrong. The gossip factor was incredible once women got together with mud, or whatever it was, on their faces. Although he would never admit it, Barry booked manicures for himself to gain entry. Usually just a nail buffing, but being around had paid off big-time more than once.

However, today, he was more interested in the groom. Too bad he couldn't be in two places at the same time.

In the church foyer, he spotted a cluster of men listening to Paula give them some kind of instructions. Though Augustus Hargrove wasn't among them, Barry edged toward the men. As soon as Paula turned her attention to the bridesmaids, Barry began his usual interview patter along with the ceremonial flashing of the ID.

"Barry Sutton, *Dallas Press*. Do you have time to answer a few questions?" He spoke to the group at large and waited for someone to answer him.

Someone did. "Tee time is in a half hour, man."

"This won't take long." Barry took down their names and learned that they were all related to the bride. "And where is the groom?" Barry kept his smile casual and friendly.

"Gus is out front."

Okay. Paula began herding everyone outside, so Barry followed. Two stretch limos waited next to the curb. Barry knew one of the drivers, but not the other. Quickly introducing himself, he made a note of the new guy's name while the bridal party headed toward the white limo and the groom's party piled into the black stretch Lincoln Navigator—an SUV on steroids.

And behind that was an unmarked white van, prickling with antenna. Augustus stood next to it and as Barry watched, a man who might have been Gus's twin in the cold, remote department emerged.

"Oh, man, is he in trouble now," said someone from inside the limo.

Still watching the groom and the other man, Barry bent down. "Who's that?"

"Derek. He's the best man."

Okay. Now things were cooking. Barry straightened and intended to approach the two men, but their body language stopped him. The groom was not happy—understandable, but the best man wasn't looking any too thrilled, either.

And that van. Barry swallowed a snicker. Why didn't they just paint a big sign on the side that said Surveillance Van? Anybody who watched any cop show on TV would know what the best man was driving.

That was one tense conversation going on beside the van. Barry took a couple of steps back and tried to melt into the giggling bridesmaids who were taking pictures of themselves by their limo, but kept an eye on the men.

Shaking his head, Gus strode toward the Navigator limo.

"Hey!" The best man—Derek—grabbed his arm and Gus promptly shook it off. "A few hours max."

"I'm getting married," Gus called back.

"Not until tomorrow," Derek said.

Their eyes locked.

Barry tried to extricate himself from the bridesmaids, but they'd asked him to take a group photo. It took a few seconds, but in that time, Derek must have convinced Gus to do whatever it was he wanted him to do because when Barry handed back the camera and looked toward the other limo, the two men were walking together toward the pin-cushion van.

Barry made a note of the license-plate number, then watched as the best man and the groom got into the van and the limos pulled away without them.

The groomsmen were headed to the Water Oaks Country Club for an afternoon of golf. The van was following their limo, but Barry didn't know if Gus and Derek were going to the country club or not. He suspected not.

The white limo pulled away and Barry stared after it, torn. According to Paula's schedule, the girls were going to spend the afternoon at the Alabaster Day Spa. Another top-notch place, a favorite of old Dallas society. He got on his cell phone and wheedled a nail-buffing appointment in an hour and a half with a nail-tech intern, and counted himself lucky to get it. He should have called a lot earlier and would have done so if the groom situation hadn't distracted him.

Well, he had an hour and a half to wait. For a nanosecond, Barry wrestled between following his reporter's intuition and doing the job he was supposed to be doing, before getting into his own car and gently rolling out of the parking lot. Burning rubber was for teenagers.

It didn't take him long to catch up with the limo and the van. Barry rode along for a couple of blocks, almost convinced that they were all going to the golf course and Gus was riding with Derek just to have a private conversation when the van suddenly turned onto a side street. No signal, no nothing. Barry was caught off guard. That turn was something else. Barry had a split second to continue following the limo, or deliberately follow the van. It wasn't as though he were driving a nondescript car, so they'd know he was behind them, but the two men couldn't know he suspected them of...well, something.

Before he could decide what to do, his hands, all by themselves, turned the wheel of his car. He was following the groom.

And he did a bang-up job, considering they went faster and faster and red lights became more suggestions than actual rules. This wasn't good. Barry didn't like traffic tickets. And he didn't want to antagonize the cops, since they'd proven to be a good source of material in the past and he was still trying to mend fences there. And yet, as the speedometer inched past the speed limit—then galloped past it— he kept up with the van.

Ah, the adrenaline rush of a breaking story. He missed this.

And then the van pulled a maneuver straight out of the *Action Movie Stunt Guide for Beginners*. Maybe *Intermediates*. It ran up onto the median, pulled a U-turn against a red light and entered traffic on the other side.

There was no way Barry was taking his car over the curb. He couldn't believe the van had made it. Swiveling around, he watched the van slip through a strip-center parking lot and down a service alley behind the stores until honking cars alerted him that the light had changed. By the time Barry managed to get his car over to the other side of the street, he'd lost the van.

Lost the van. Lost a big, solid white van that gleamed in the afternoon sunlight. Man, was he rusty.

Barry parked his car. Okay, now what? There was something going on. He knew it. And he wanted to find out what. *Needed* to find out what.

He'd been a good boy and had taken his punishment for months, which was how long it had been since he'd sunk his teeth into a story meatier than caterers jacking up prices when it was too late to book anyone else.

He stared at the van's license-plate number and tapped his notebook. What was with the best man? No one seemed to know him—they barely knew the groom. Barry checked the wedding info he'd been given for a last name. There it was. Best Man: Derek Stafford.

It would be interesting to find out about those two, and it *was* his job to write about the wedding party. Details, his new editor was constantly carping.

So she wanted details. Barry checked his Palm. Who in the police department could run the license plate for him? Stephanie? No. They'd dated and it had ended badly. Didn't it always? Gina? Maybe. Barry had maintained his contacts as best he could, but even he had to admit that the atmosphere in the police department was chilly these days.

His last story had been an incredible piece of detective work. It had just been published too early, that's all. But nobody held a grudge like a cop.

Barry mentally sussed out the Dallas squad room,

eliminating the men—he'd taken enough guff from them over the society reporting—and settled on Megan. There had always been an unacknowledged *something* between them. The question of who was going to acknowledge it first and when added a nice zing to their dealings.

Barry had to admit that he missed seeing Megan at briefings more than he missed the briefings. In the cynical world of journalism, she'd been a beacon of honesty. She'd made him believe when he hadn't wanted to. How corny was that?

Way too corny. He had to push the zing aside and snap out of it. The point was that Megan was his best bet to run the plate. He sent her a quick e-mail.

2

Megan Esterbrook stared at her computer screen. The nerve! Her squeak of outrage alerted Gina, a fellow policewoman whose desk faced hers.

In answer to Gina's arched eyebrow, Megan opened and closed her mouth inarticulately, then pointed a finger at her computer monitor.

"What?"

Megan stared at the return e-mail address and felt her hands sweat and her heart pound. How intensely annoying. Not trusting herself to speak, she jabbed her finger at the computer screen again.

From where she sat, Gina couldn't see Megan's screen. After walking around the desks, she stood next to Megan's chair. "Barry."

"Yes!" Megan hissed. "He e-mailed me!"

"So I see."

Gina apparently failed to understand the depth of Barry's perfidy.

"How can Barry Sutton just expect me to ignore the fact that he's the reason I've been banished to a desk for months?"

"Hit the delete key. Problem solved."

Yes, that would be the logical thing to do. Megan

could pretend she never got it. E-mails went astray all the time. And yet just the appearance of Barry's name made her heart pound harder than it ever did with her police work. Maybe that's because she was trained for police work. Nothing had trained her for Barry.

"Megan?" Gina prompted. "We've talked about this."

"I know."

"Deep breaths."

"I know."

"Now hit delete."

She made it sound so easy. "I—"

Gina leaned over, her finger headed for Megan's delete key. Megan grabbed her wrist.

"Megan!"

"I know he's only e-mailing me because he wants something." And not because he'd suddenly developed a grand passion for her, she didn't say aloud. And from Gina's expression, Megan figured she didn't have to.

"And you know what happens when Barry asks for favors?"

"I give them to him. And bad things happen," Megan recited in a monotone.

"Very good. Delete the e-mail."

Megan stared at Barry's name. "How can he make me feel guilty when he's the one asking for a favor?"

"Because that's what he does." Gina spoke in slow, measured tones—her "talk them off the ledge" voice. "He is an expert. He's like a legit con man. You've studied them. You know how they read and manipulate people."

Megan nodded, her eyes never leaving the "Barry Sutton" on the e-mail. "You know he has different smiles?"

"Most of us—"

"Not like Barry. I know he's practiced them and cataloged them. I've watched him watching other people. Then he'll paste a smile on his face and approach them. You see, he always smiles first. He decides how he's going to appear. He can make himself have dimples, or not. He regulates how much of his teeth he shows. It's never spontaneous. And once you respond to him, that's the smile you always get. You know what mine is?"

Gina carefully shook her head. Her eyes had widened slightly, as though she thought she was dealing with a crazy person. Maybe she was.

Megan continued anyway. "I get the single-dimple smile with the slightly lowered brow. A pseudo-private smile, as though there's something between us that no one else knows about. Then, after I helplessly blab everything he wants to know, he takes one side of his mouth down a notch and flashes the other dimple. And then he winks. I hate winking. Hate it. But he's always turned away by then. Once I told not to wink at me and he just gave me a double-dimpled smile and said he knew I loved it."

Gina stared at her. "Have you been practicing your Barry aversion therapy?"

"Sort of." It just made Megan think of him more.

"Now would be a good time."

She was really lucky Gina was being so patient with her. Megan felt so gullible and so stupid and so silly and so *weak* when it came to Barry. But Gina said everyone had weaknesses. She, herself, couldn't speak in public. Appearing on camera the way Megan had—before her reassignment—made Gina freeze up. Megan had seen Gina in action, or nonaction, so she knew it was true. It was Gina, who had studied psychology, who'd helped her devise the Barry aversion therapy.

Megan slid open her desk drawer and withdrew a set of lined index cards. On each was written one of Barry's transgressions.

"Read one aloud," Gina instructed.

Megan drew a breath. "He smiles at me even though he knows it makes my face go all red."

"What is it with you and the smiling?"

"People will think there's something going on between us!" Megan defended herself.

"Oh, please. Get over yourself and give me that card." Gina took it and tore it up. "There are plenty of other more serious consequences to dealing with Barry, and you know it." She pointed to the stack of cards. "Write another one—write that his requests for special treatment disrupt your peace of mind and affect your work."

"They don't affect my work!"

"Have we not just spent ten minutes obsessing over Barry?"

"It's not obsessing."

Gina nodded toward the computer. "Delete the e-mail."

Megan swallowed. "I...should read it first."

Gina leveled her stern policewoman's stare at Megan. "Deep breath. Read the next card."

Megan inhaled and exhaled. "Barry called me in the middle of the night—"

"At your unlisted home number."

Megan hoped that Gina wouldn't ask how Barry got her unlisted home number. "He knew I would be asleep," she continued, "and took advantage of my grogginess to trick me into giving him the mayor's meeting schedule, which then confirmed that the mayor was meeting with out-of-state candidates for the new assistant police chief." An echo of the anger she'd felt then calmed her pounding heart now. Hey, this aversion-therapy stuff might work.

"It was a dirty trick, but it was very clever," Gina commented.

"I still should have been prepared."

"He woke you up at one-thirty in the morning! On purpose!"

"He had a deadline."

"You are *not* defending him."

Megan stared at the card. She *was* defending him, drat it all. "Okay. You're right. Thanks, Gina. I can handle things now."

"You're deleting the e-mail?"

"I'm going to write a refusal before I open and read it."

"Megan—"

"Gina." Megan stiffened her spine. "I have no business deleting e-mails unread. If I do, then he *is* affecting my work. I have to be able to deal with him when I'm department spokeswoman again. This is good practice."

Gina gave her a look with just a touch of pity in it, then headed back to her own desk.

Pity, huh? Megan brought her fingers to the keyboard, mentally composing a polite, yet firm, very firm, refusal, when another e-mail from Barry popped up with the subject line *Need urgent favor.*

The sinking feeling she tried to ignore told her that she'd been hoping the first e-mail might be a let's-get-together-for-coffee e-mail. Which would be a prelude to a dinner or a movie or a night of wild monkey sex.

No!

She did not think that way ever. Certainly not about Barry. Okay, she would not think that way about Barry ever again. Gritting her teeth, Megan tried to type a scathing reply to the as-yet unread message, but her hands had been sweating and *SDeR B Atty* was all she managed to type.

Oh, fine. Sighing, she opened the e-mails and discovered that he wanted her to run a license-plate number for him. He was interested in a name and whether that name dinged any police bells.

Although cops had been known to do so, accessing the Law Enforcement Information Network outside the performance of official duties was totally against the rules and Megan wasn't in a position to break any rules. She typed back a naked *No* and hit Send, feeling strongly virtuous.

The feeling lasted for a couple of seconds before she realized she'd made a tactical error.

"Oh, no."

"What?" Gina asked.

"I shouldn't have answered him."

"You *answered* him?"

"I said, 'No.'" Megan's e-mail was already chiming. "But now he knows I'm here."

"What did he want?"

"For me to run a plate."

Shaking her head, Gina pointedly looked at her monitor. "I didn't hear that."

"It's okay that you heard it. I'm not going to do it."

Gina didn't meet her eyes.

"I'm not!" Megan had to raise her voice over the sound of the e-mail chime. She turned off the sound.

She tried very hard to concentrate on her very important work—yes, the world would be a better place once she finished inventorying the True Blue pencils that the community relations department passed out to school kids. She was about to make a huge decision: The navy-night color was no longer manufactured so Megan had been given the responsibility of choosing a new color for their next order. It was important. It was. Every time elementary school students used their pencils, they'd think of the police. The blue—and yes, it would stay blue—color had to be strong, but not intimidating. She had a call into the Dallas Cowboys organization to find out what their shade of blue was called so the police didn't duplicate it. But the police had gold lettering and the Cowboys had silver, so Megan thought that was enough of a difference if their only choice was the Cowboys' blue—well, the point was, she was busy making important decisions here. She had no time to pay attention to Barry and his incessant e-mails.

They were coming at the rate of one a minute now. What a jerk.

And then three minutes went by without one and Megan was lured into looking at them and their identical subject lines: *I'm sorry. Please?*

Megan slumped. Honestly, for all the mental energy she'd expended, she should just— No. This was a test and if she gave in now, she would never be able to take a stand against him again.

A thought occurred to her and she grabbed for her phone and activated the instant voice mail. He'd be calling any minute.

She wouldn't be able to keep her voice mail set that way for long, but Barry wasn't stupid. He'd get the message and leave her alone.

She waited, then went back online to search the Internet for pencils.

She had three solid minutes to compare pencil colors and quantity prices before her e-mail icon flashed. The subject line read *You're not answering your phone.*

Megan sighed.

"You could block his e-mails," Gina suggested.

"I hate myself," Megan muttered. "He just... just..."

"Pushes all your buttons?"

"Oh, it's worse than that. I have special buttons just for him."

Chuckling, Gina leaned down and when she straightened, she handed Megan a handful of change across their desks. "I could use a Dr Pepper right now. You could, too."

"Yes. Dr Pepper. Sugar. Caffeine." Megan stood. "I'm on it."

"Why, thank you, Megan." Gina grinned and pointed to her dimples.

Megan's e-mail chimed.

"I thought you turned that off."

"It turns on after you access it."

"Oh, Megan."

"I'm going now."

"Good idea."

Megan used the walk to the break room to clear her mind of Barry Sutton and his e-mails. The squad room was packed with officers and detectives. Why did he pick on her?

Because she was a soft touch, Megan thought, answering her own question. She had no business being a soft touch. She was a police officer. She was competent and in control.

Megan shoved quarters into the soda machine and took a restorative swallow as soon as she opened the can. Okay. Technically, Barry was harassing her. Therefore, she would send him an e-mail explaining exactly what the consequences were if he didn't cease and desist because if she received one more e-mail, she was turning him in. Strong. Competent. No nonsense.

When she got back to her desk, there were fifty-seven e-mails clogging her in-box and they were now arriving every few seconds.

Megan sent her cease-and-desist e-mail and then waited.

They stopped.

"Quitter," she muttered, almost disappointed.

Twenty minutes later, Barry strode across the squad room.

BARRY DID NOT HAVE time for this, but apparently Megan was the type to hold a grudge and would require a little face-to-face intervention.

Frankly, he was surprised. Usually, getting Megan to cooperate was a no-brainer. She was refreshingly eager to please, so honest she squeaked, and had both freckles and breasts. Barry had figured out that she liked the freckles and didn't know what to do with the breasts. She was the type of woman who felt they got in the way. And he supposed they did. They sure spoiled the line of her uniform. And he meant that in a good way.

She was sun-kissed cute, the type of girl a guy would ask to fill in on a Saturday softball game. Barry didn't play softball, but he could appreciate her type. He'd decided her type was the adolescent pal who suddenly developed a sexy little body that she ignored and none of her guy pals could. The way to her heart was to ignore her womanly charms and treat her like a kid sister—somebody else's kid sister. See, that kind of subtlety was the key to Barry's success. If he treated her like *his* kid sister, then the male-female thing was not there. Somebody else's kid sister, and the male-female thing *could* be there. It was that whiff of possibility that he put into the smile he reserved just for her.

Yeah, Barry thought he had her pegged and yet

she wouldn't answer her phone or her e-mails. He figured maybe he hadn't groveled enough. For a straight arrow like Megan, being reprimanded had clearly cut deep. He should have acknowledged that.

That was a mistake on his part. He'd apologized repeatedly in the e-mails, and he also had back when he'd heard she'd been reassigned, but he should have made more of an effort. Flowers, or something. Except she wasn't the flowers sort. Anyway, he'd been too preoccupied with his own situation to give it much thought. Now he knew he should have followed up with her so that he could have salvaged their professional relationship.

Barry learned from his mistakes. He wouldn't make that one again.

Megan always spoke the truth. She was the best thing to ever happen to the Dallas police force—but she was dangerous to the media. Yes, she absolutely spoke the truth—as she knew it—and Barry suspected it was just a matter of time before someone exploited her.

Megan was too honorable to see dishonor in someone else. Some people might call that naïveté, but Barry admired her faith in her fellow human beings, even as he knew that he'd have exploited her long before now.

He wasn't proud of that. Just realistic.

So when Megan didn't respond to his e-mail entreaties, he knew this whole mess had changed her. He profoundly regretted that—and was surprised he hadn't caught it on his previous trips back to the squad room.

Well, he was here to make things right, now.

And to get that plate run.

He scanned the room and discovered that the setup hadn't changed since the last time he'd made the rounds here. He acknowledged the faces he recognized, acutely aware that his reception might best be described as "cool" and turned his attention toward Megan.

He caught a glare from what's-her-name—Gina, the Italian who never smiled at him—and nodded at her before focusing on Megan. Slowly, he smiled their special smile.

MEGAN HAD BEEN half expecting him, but that still didn't lessen Barry's impact on her psyche. She gave up trying to ignore him and just propped her chin in her hand and watched him sail around the islands of clustered desks in the squad-room sea. He was headed for her. The smile clinched it, if she'd had any doubt.

She might as well enjoy the view.

It wasn't that Barry was stunningly handsome, it was that he was interestingly handsome. His nose was on the large side, as noses went, but it fit his face, due to his strong jaw. There was watchful intelligence in his eyes and Megan doubted she'd ever seen a genuine, uncalculated emotion in them.

She allowed herself a tiny exhale. This crush she had on Barry was so annoying. She was to the point of wanting to throw herself at him and let him use her until he tired of her, which was extremely unhealthy. She wouldn't do it in a million years. But she wanted to, which was bad enough.

And her crush had obviously distracted her to the point that she'd let slip some crucial piece of information last fall. She had gone over and over what she'd said to him during that fateful press conference. That part had been taped. But afterward, reporters had approached her and, because Megan knew they were doing their jobs and because she didn't have anything to hide, she'd informally answered a few questions.

To be honest, she'd known Barry would be one of the reporters to approach her. He always tried for the extra bit of information. It was a pathetic way to be closer to him but her pathetic heart craved it because for some unknown pathetic reason, he brightened her pathetic life. Pathetic, that's what it was. Utterly pathetic. Like the way she was watching him right now. Pathetic. He was watching her, too, and knew the effect he had on her. She'd seen that particular smile often enough that she could see behind it sometimes. Right now, satisfaction was behind it. He thought he had her. And maybe he did.

For pity's sake, the man even looked good in fluorescent light! She didn't have a chance. She was Custer at Little Big Horn, Napoleon at Waterloo, the *Titanic* kissing an iceberg.

He wore his standard uniform of sports jacket and tie, which should have looked out of place in these days of casual attire but didn't. He covered the casual aspect with a perfectly fitted pair of jeans.

Without breaking eye contact, Megan slid open her desk drawer, keeping her note cards at the ready.

She didn't actually have to read them, but it was a good idea to have them in sight.

"Hey, Megan." He approached, his aura brightening the drabness of her desk area.

"Barry."

Hands in his pockets, he tilted his head to one side and gave her the other half of her smile—and she hadn't even done what he wanted yet. This was a first. She waited, and yes, here was the lowered head with the just-between-us look. The wink was next. She hoped he wouldn't wink at her. It was so fake. So contrived. People didn't wink in real life. Well, other than gangsters winking at little girls in white-lace dresses just after giving them ice-cream cones. Or old men and really, really young women who were blond and really, really stacked. Or cowboys. Cowboys winked, come to think of it.

But Barry was none of those things and, therefore, not entitled to wink.

Megan should look away—specifically toward the drawer with the note cards.

Since she couldn't look away, she should at least say something. Anything. Anything to head off the wink. But what was there to say?

Barry winked.

"Don't do that," Megan burst out crossly.

"Don't do what?"

"Wink."

"You like the wink."

"No! I don't!"

"Sure you do."

"No, really. I hate winking. It makes you look smarmy."

He gazed at her, looking fake-affronted. "Smarmy? As I understand the definition of smarmy, I am not smarmy. I am anti-smarm."

"Then don't wink."

He leaned forward, just a little bit, but most definitely crossing the invisible bubble of her personal space. "It's okay that you like it."

Megan gritted her teeth, drawing on all her public-appearance experience. "I do not like it. It makes me feel patronized. Belittled. Suckered."

Barry's face went blank. Honestly, he looked like a living computer reprogramming itself. She must have convinced him and now he was updating her file. Megan Esterbrook—delete wink.

He gave her a considering look and plucked a rolling office chair from a nearby empty computer station, twirled it around and straddled it, crossing his hands along the back and resting his chin on top.

They were now eye to eye and his were blue and crinkled at the corners when he smiled. He was studying her. Analyzing her and figuring out his next approach. Look at him—not even bothering to hide what he was doing.

Megan tried to keep her expression blank, but she could feel her face heating up and knew it was a lost cause. At least could she try to hide the fact that she had this enormous thing for him? No, apparently not. Honestly, this crush of hers qualified as a disability.

"Why are you just now telling me you didn't like the wink?"

"I told you before. You didn't hear me."

"You could have told me again."

"You never stuck around. It was smile, wink and poof." She snapped her fingers. "You were gone."

"Next time I'll wait before poofing."

A smile tugged at the corners of her mouth, but she was determined not to give in. "Why are you here, Barry?"

But she knew. Might as well get this over with.

"I'm here in a public-service capacity. Your e-mail is down."

"Yes. Someone spammed my in-box."

He was still trying to read her and she was afraid he would read more than she wanted him to.

His face wasn't exactly blank anymore. It had softened. Gentled. It looked honest, or as honest as she suspected Barry ever got. Not that he was dishonest, as far as she knew, but he didn't reveal anything of himself. Right now, he was focused completely on her.

How often did that happen—a man focusing completely on a woman? On her? Who cared enough to make the effort to please her, never mind what for?

She wanted to melt. Actually, she quite possibly could already be melting—when was the last time she'd felt her toes? She just wanted to fling herself at him, and kiss him senseless. Since she'd knock over the chair in the process, she'd probably have a better chance of rendering herself senseless.

Megan knew Barry would never approach her in a sexual way. There were women far more approachable than she. Women who knew how to look like sexy women, not women who wore jogging bras under police uniforms.

If she didn't stop thinking of him this way, she'd explode. Lust was explosive, wasn't it?

Maybe they'd all find out pretty quick.

"You're still mad at me." He hadn't changed expressions.

"What? Oh. I'm not mad at you as much as I'm mad at myself."

"Don't be. I'm not mad at myself. I did my job."

Megan exhaled. "I didn't do mine."

"Yeah, you did. I had a couple of lucky guesses."

"It was more than luck."

"Luck and experience." And he gave her a wry smile—one corner of his mouth twisted and then he pressed his lips together. It was uncalculated. A genuine Barry expression. Wow.

And it got to her. She was going to have to sit on her hands or she would grab him and kiss that mouth.

"Run the plate for me?" Still the wry smile.

Damn it! He'd seen how she'd responded. Oh, great. That was going to be her new smile, she guessed, unless she put a stop to it right now.

"No."

"Please?" His voice was husky. Intimate. Dangerous.

"Hey. We're not allowed to access the program just on a whim. I could get into serious trouble here and I don't have to remind you that I'm already in serious trouble. I spent six months on desk detail.

Even now, I'm only being sent to schools and giving safety lectures to neighborhood groups. I—"

"I'm covering the Shipley-Hargrove wedding. The groom is not where he should be."

Megan straightened. This was serious. A civilian was reporting a crime and she'd—

"Stop the panic." Barry grimaced. "I'm working on a hunch. The groom didn't like being photographed and then he takes off with the best man who was driving a standard-issue surveillance van. I have the plate number. I just wondered if he's okay."

"Are you talking...kidnapped?"

"I don't know what I'm talking. This is a big-deal wedding with some big-deal guests." Barry reached into his jacket breast pocket. "Here's the wedding guest list. If I can't know names, just tell me if the name from the plate is on the guest list."

There was a loud clearing of a throat. Gina raised her eyebrows.

Megan had forgotten about Gina. She'd forgotten about everybody. Except Barry.

"Is this man bothering you?" Gina asked.

"Give me a break, Gina," Barry murmured.

Gina leveled a look at Megan and opened and closed her desk drawer.

Right. Megan turned to him. "If you feel a crime has been committed, then you should report it to—"

"No way." Barry stood. "You're the officer I've approached."

"But it's not my duty—"

"Don't you guys have to follow the Hippocratic oath?"

"That's doctors, and stop interrupting me."

Barry sat back down and wheeled his chair next to hers. Leaning forward, he spoke in a voice so soft that Megan had to lean in close just to hear him. Not exactly a hardship.

"Megan, I'm a desperate man. It's been seven months since I've been allowed to cover hard news. I've been stuck in lace-covered, sugarcoated, rose-scented hell. I think there's hard news here and I don't want the story going to anyone else."

Megan opened and closed her mouth.

"I'll let you know everything I find out. You'll be the spokeswoman again. Let me make it up to you, Megan. Let me make it right."

The man could charm bark from a tree. The thought of representing the Dallas police once again made Megan's mouth water.

"Just a name." She turned away so she wouldn't know if triumph flashed in those blue eyes or not.

He was entitled.

After a few moments, she had information. "The van's registered to a Sterling International."

"Never heard of them. Got an address?"

"A PO box."

Barry took out his notebook. "There's gotta be a street address for deliveries."

Megan punched a couple of buttons. Info was pretty skimpy on Sterling International. "No street addy that I can find at this level." She waited because she knew Barry was going to—

"Then go to the next level," he ordered impatiently.

"Megan—" Warning sounded in Gina's voice.

"Everybody just calm down." Megan took a breath and released it. "I've already been to the next level. Nada. I'm not authorized to go any farther, so I've Googled it. Wanna see?"

Barry rolled his chair right next to hers. He still wore the same light cottony sea-breezy scent and whether it was from the soap he used or a fragrance he applied, Megan knew it was chosen to be on the pleasant side of neutral.

Or maybe it was just fabric softener.

"Scroll."

Megan scrolled. Barry whistled and pointed. "Click that one."

Megan clicked. A garishly dark-colored over-the-top warning page appeared on her monitor.

"Click past that."

"Now wait a minute—it says my computer will be traced and the police will flag it."

"You *are* the police."

"All the more reason—"

"Come on, Megan." He barely whispered it.

His breath teased the hairs on her neck. She shivered and clicked, then leaned back and let Barry take control of the computer mouse. "That's one of those conspiracy theory Web sites."

"Hmm." He was clicking faster than Megan could read.

"You know, Sterling isn't that unusual a name. You probably have the wrong one."

"Maybe." Barry sat back and checked his watch. "Well, this is all very fascinating, but I want to check out Sterling International in person and see if I can find the groom. Since we don't have a street address, I'm going to go to the post office where this box is located and check out the area."

Megan closed her eyes. She should just wave him away. But she didn't. "Hang on and let me try something."

She could feel Gina staring at her, but didn't glance up.

And then she could feel Barry looking at her. Not watching her screen, but looking at her. She didn't glance up for him, either.

Megan had to search several commercial property lists before she found what she was looking for, but she finally did get an address for Sterling International.

She wrote it down on one of the True Blue for You notepads she gave out when she spoke at schools. "Try this. It's from census archives. It might not be any good, but at least it's something."

"Thanks, sweet cheeks." And he kissed her. Right on the cheek.

Megan stopped breathing so she could fully experience the brief encounter with Barry's lips. There wasn't a lot to experience.

Barry, already on his feet, bestowed her one-dimpled smile on her and Megan braced herself.

So did Barry. With an amused shake of his head, he stood, waiting for a response.

Megan reluctantly waggled her fingers at him and he responded with a two-fingered salute before striding through the squad room.

It was probably going to be their new routine. Megan sighed and noticed Gina watching her.

"Oh, be quiet," she muttered.

"Did I say anything?" Eyebrows raised, Gina continued typing.

Megan stared at the index cards in her open drawer and sighed. She was hopeless. Utterly hopeless. Rather than banging her head on her desk, Megan withdrew a blank card and wrote, "Give in." If nothing else worked, she might as well keep her options open.

3

STERLING INTERNATIONAL was located in an office building that required Barry to hand over ID to a security guard who photographed it before Barry was allowed to enter the elevator.

The dark oak door with the heavy brass lettering—very expensive-looking—was locked. Sure it was a Friday afternoon, but it was still business hours. Someone should be manning the phones, unless the sole proprietor was out driving a white van somewhere. Barry knocked, not really expecting a response, and he didn't get one.

He looked up and down the hall at the entrances to the other three businesses. Their doors had glass in them. The one on the opposite side of the hall was all glass and surrounded by glass walls. Glass was very friendly. The receptionist looked equally friendly. Barry entered the reception area and smiled a full-out aren't-you-a-sexy-little-number smile. He was careful dispensing that kind of smile, what with all the prickly women taking offense at everything these days, but she melted like butter on hot biscuits. Truly gratifying. After Megan, Barry's self-confidence needed bolstering.

Megan hating the wink had seriously jarred his inner Zen. He'd carefully remembered to wink after every encounter and had never got a negative vibe until now. He'd misread her at some point and hadn't realized because he'd never tried to read her again. He'd become complacent and unobservant and too dependent on the underlying zing. Not good.

But now he, thanks to Tiffani-with-an-*i*, knew that the Sterling International folks kept to themselves— when they were there at all. Nobody knew much about them, and Tiffani, who had a clear view of the hallway, never noticed much traffic going in and out.

Sounded like a company fronting for something else. Barry still could be making a lot out of nothing, but he didn't think so.

Back in his car, Barry sat in the parking lot and opened his laptop, thinking again that wireless Internet was the greatest invention ever, or at least since the cell phone. A little poking around in Derek Stafford's background revealed nothing. Placeholder stuff. In fact, this background was very similar to the groom's. It was a government whitewash background.

Cool. This was a heck of a lot more interesting than getting the flower girl's name spelled correctly. Anyway, all the little girls had bizarre names these days. When he had a little girl, he was naming her Elizabeth. The name was ancient, had a great history and could be twisted into anything the girl wished. Liz, Beth, Betty, Liza, Lizzie, Isabel, Eliza, Betsy, Ellie. Every girl should be named Elizabeth.

Megan was probably a form of Elizabeth, because he was thinking that was a good name, too.

Focus. Barry usually didn't have to corral his wandering attention. Weddings had corrupted him. Swimming in estrogen soup had affected his brain. That had to be it.

So. He needed more information because all his reporter antennae were on alert. Something was going on. Guys like Gus and Derek didn't do fancy weddings for marrying purposes. They were low-key guys.

And how about little Sally? Was staid and elegant her style? Not from what Barry knew. So what was up? Was this a faux wedding? Had Sally finally gone over the edge, been caught, and this was a plea bargain? The government wanted to use her society standing and fake a wedding to cover something else?

Barry loved this kind of stuff. He could kiss Sally himself. He got out the guest list again. Glittering. All the jewels of Dallas society—and there was the congressman right in the middle of it all. Yeah, yeah, he was a friend of the bride's family—and it didn't hurt that the wedding was in his constituency, either. Galloway would never turn down positive press.

And another clue—where were the friends and family of the groom? And how would a woman like Sally meet Gus, anyway? And why would he be attracted to her? Sure she was a looker, but c'mon. This was Dallas. Lots o' lookers in Dallas.

Barry shook his head. He really needed to be with the bride and ask questions. The chatter at the spa was probably loaded.

And yet, he had a feeling the story was with the groom, wherever he was. Maybe by now, he was at the country club and if Barry didn't check out Water Oaks, the trail would grow cold.

It was just after two-thirty and his nail buffing was at three. Golf...spa. Golf...spa...

Megan. Oh, yeah. Megan would help him out. He'd ditch the wink and she wouldn't be able to resist him. Smiling to himself, he e-mailed her a thank-you for the information. And then he offered her a little treat.

MEGAN STARED AT HER E-MAIL, mouth agape. Barry thanking her was weird enough, but a manicure? How had he come up with that? She narrowed her eyes suspiciously. There had to be a trick here, but she couldn't figure it out.

"Gina? What kind of man gives a woman a manicure as a thank-you gift?"

"Lots of guys—"

"I'm talking unmarried men. Men in noncommitted relationships or even no relationships."

Gina gave her a "you're kidding" look, then seemed to understand. "Oh, you mean girlie men, right?"

"Ya think Barry's a girlie man?"

Gina goggled at her. "Barry's giving you a manicure? Just when you think you've heard everything."

"Well, he's not offering to do it *himself*."

"But still...can you imagine one of the guys around here giving you a thank-you manicure?"

No, she couldn't. "Then it's not just me. It's kind of a weird thing."

"Unless..." Gina stretched to see around her monitor. "Let's see those nails, girlfriend."

Megan held up her hands with their short, no-nonsense nails. They looked fine to her.

And apparently to Gina. "You got me." Gina shrugged. "Whatever it is, Barry wants something."

"For sure. Maybe he's investigating slave labor or spa health-code violations and needs somebody to test them."

"Nail Fungus," Gina intoned. "Society's Secret Shame."

Megan laughed and typed back an e-mail. "I'm asking him where," she told Gina.

He responded instantly. "Omigosh, it's at the Alabaster Spa."

"Wow." Gina looked impressed. "He must want something big."

"Or maybe it's nothing more than a thank-you the way he says it is."

They stared at each other, then laughed. "Nah."

Gina shrugged. "It's a free manicure at the Alabaster. I'd go for it."

"I've never had a manicure," Megan said as she e-mailed her acceptance.

Great! Pick you up in ten minutes, said the answering e-mail.

Megan blinked at it. "No! He can't do that." He was manipulating her again and she was letting him. When would she ever learn?

"What?" Gina looked alarmed.

"He's picking me up in ten minutes. I thought maybe somebody gave him a gift certificate or something and he was passing it along to me. I can't just up and leave."

Gina pointed at the clock. "Our watch ends at three. I'll cover the last few minutes for you."

Megan hadn't realized it was so close to three o'clock. "I don't know. There might be a pencil emergency. Can you stand the pressure?"

"Go have a manicure."

Megan wanted to. She'd never gotten the hang of all this girl stuff. It had always seemed like so much effort. When she'd started appearing on camera, she'd quickly learned the value of makeup, but it wasn't something that ever felt natural to her and she never thought she was applying it right. Still, a light hand was better than no hand. Speaking of hands… she looked down at her fingers. Oh, why not? Besides, she'd already told him yes.

Barry arrived before her watch ended. "Hop chop. Your appointment is at three."

"You know you could have asked fir—"

"I'm covering for her," Gina interrupted.

Barry flashed one of his megawatt grins in her direction. "Thanks, Gina."

Megan was slightly gratified to see Gina blink once before nodding. It wasn't much of a reaction, but the fact that Gina had reacted at all made Megan feel less weak. Barry was a manly force to be reckoned with, that's all.

"I'll drive myself," Megan told him.

"We can take my car. My treat." But he narrowed his eyes.

"What?"

"The uniform…" He wiggled his hand from side to side. "I dunno."

"I've got clothes in the locker room," Megan heard herself say when she hadn't intended to say anything of the sort.

"Go for it. And hurry up." He looked back at Gina and sat on the corner of her desk. "In the meantime, I'll hang with Gina."

Megan hurried and it wasn't because he was "hanging with Gina," either. It wasn't.

She was still going to drive her own car, though. With Barry, it was always best to have some control. And a method of escape.

At least that's what she thought until she saw Barry's car. It was a blue vintage Mustang. "Oh, cool."

"You like?" Barry rubbed at an imaginary spot on the gleaming finish.

"Did you restore it yourself?"

"I..." He sucked his breath between his teeth. "No. I bought it this way. But I would have restored it if I'd had the time. And the knowledge," he admitted.

And here she'd been revising her opinion of him. "Pop the hood."

"You'll be late for your manicure."

Megan raised an eyebrow. Maybe he *was* a girlie man. "Come on. I want to see what she's got."

"The Alabaster Spa is not the place to play looseygoosey with time." He pointed to his watch. "And we're pushing it as it is."

But Megan released the hood latch. How could he not want to show off his engine? "It's been a long time since I've seen a carburetor."

"Yeah." Impatience radiated from him.

The fact that he didn't want to talk cars with her

told Megan more than anything that he wanted
something from her.

"We need to get a move on."

Megan grinned up at him as she bent over the engine and poked at a couple of hoses and jiggled the
idle arm. She wiped at a grease smear on the back of
her hand as she straightened. "Relax. I sure won't be
able to do this *after* the manicure."

Barry shook his head. "Am I the only one who
thinks this conversation is surreal? You want to talk
cars and I'm talking manicures?"

Megan laughed as she dug in the pocket of her
hoodie for a tissue. She closed the hood, and then
wiped off her fingers. "Okay, we can go. But you're
going to have to tell me what's up sometime."

"I don't want them to skimp on the arm massage
because you're late, that's all."

"Oh, right. The all-important arm massage."
Megan rolled her eyes.

Barry opened the door for her and waved her inside. "You've never had a manicure."

Megan got inside the car. "I can paint my own
nails when I want to."

"Do you ever want to?"

"I'm usually too busy."

Megan didn't know if Barry heard her since he
carefully shut the door, as though she'd do something crass like slam it.

He jogged around the front of the car, glancing at
his watch again.

Megan wished she'd thought to bring her index
cards. She had a feeling she was going to need them.

As they drove away from the curb, Megan realized that this was the first time she'd been alone with Barry—*alone* alone. He kept up an innocuous chatter—the man could talk about anything—that didn't require any deep thought on her part. It did give her a good excuse to look at him, which made this whole trip worth it. She might as well indulge in a fantasy, or two. Barry wouldn't know that she was admiring the line of his jaw or wondering what kind of a kisser he was. He ought to be pretty good, considering how much exercise his mouth got.

Megan considered finding out the next time he stopped at a traffic signal. Maybe she should just lean across the gearbox and plant one on him. It wasn't her style, but what did she have to lose, really? Not Barry. And he was too smooth to shove her away or act repulsed. No, he'd find a classy way of disengaging—maybe even after returning her kiss for a moment.

Megan drew in a deep breath. That could be some moment. Undoubtedly worth the subsequent embarrassment. Barry would probably avoid her then, but wouldn't that make her life a lot easier?

"Megan?"

"Hmm?"

"You're staring."

"You're talking."

"Am I boring you?"

"No."

"So the glazed expression is a sign of extreme interest?"

"Absolutely."

Their gazes caught and held. Well, here she was having a moment and she didn't know what to do with it. Catching him by surprise with a rogue kiss was one thing; initiating a lip-lock with him looking straight at her was just not going to happen.

"Why aren't you driving?" she asked.

Barry gestured to the approaching valet. "We're here."

Good call on not kissing him. The valet yanked open her door and the springs squawked in protest. She touched Barry on the arm and leaned toward him. "Don't let them drive this car!" she ordered in a whisper.

He grinned. "Wasn't planning to." He winked, then caught himself. "Sorry."

"That's okay." She straightened. "I might change my mind about the wink."

As she got out of the car, he was still wearing a baffled half smile. All right! Megan was learning that to hold her own with Barry, she had to avoid being pigeonholed. She planned never to let him become complacent around her again.

The spa personnel all knew Barry, which didn't surprise Megan. She sat in one of the plush gray chairs and waited for the catch. There was bound to be one.

Barry had leaned over the marble reception desk and was making goo-goo eyes at the pretty receptionist, no doubt trying to talk her into something.

Megan nervously noted that every female in the place was polished and femininely confident in a way she envied. Sure it was great graduating from the police academy. Using a gun was cool. Being able to take down men twice her size was a kick, but she was a woman after all. She had all the equipment, but she couldn't figure out how to use it as these women did. She got along with men just fine and she'd had boyfriends, but among certain other women—these women, for instance—she felt uncomfortable.

Barry was one of those guys who liked feminine women. And Megan was one of those women who liked manly men, the uncomplicated, unpretentious types. The kind for whom a smile was just a smile and not a way to manipulate.

So why was Barry the guy who made her insides, not to mention her brain, turn to mush?

The mush-man crooked a finger at her as the receptionist glided away from her chair.

"Good news. Tessa can work you in for some highlights. It'll be with Noelle, who's apprenticing, but, hey, on a Friday, you're in luck."

"What are you talking about?" She eyed him suspiciously.

"Your hair."

Megan tucked a stray strand behind her ear. Her hair was in a twisted knot at the back of her neck. It was professional and out of the way and she thought it always looked good, especially if she had to put on her hat. Hat hair on TV wasn't pretty. "What about my hair?"

He gave her the new smile. She'd dub it his serious smile. "Call it another treat. I owe you."

Catch alert. "And?"

"And enjoy yourself."

"And?"

"I'll see you later." Adding the sincere pressed lips to the smile, which actually made Megan want to shake him, he turned away.

She waited. "And?" she called softly.

Finger tapping his temple as though he'd just remembered something, Barry turned back. "Well, you know, there is something—"

"I knew it. I *knew* it."

He held up his hands and backed away. "Forget it."

"What?"

"No. Just enjoy."

"Barry!"

"Okay, look." His face was all seriousness. "The Shipley wedding party is here."

Megan groaned. Yes, the precinct was all aflutter with the extra security and overtime for the big society wedding.

"If you could just—"

"I'm not bothering the bride and her bridesmaids!"

"Just talk to her."

Was he nuts? "I don't know her! I don't know any of them!"

"But you're here. They're here. You'll be getting your nails done—they'll be getting their nails done. You'll have a lot in common."

She had nothing in common with them. "Barry..."

"You know, just idle chitchat—how she met the groom, how long they've known each other, whether she knows the best man, anything about the best man, anything about the groom's family, any glitches in the plans, and—oh, yeah—does she know where in the heck the groom is?"

"You are unbelievable."

He gave her the new sincere smile. The smile she wanted to wipe off his face. "Megan…"

"Hi!" Tessa was back. "Here's Noelle. She's still in training, but a senior stylist will supervise."

"So, we're doing highlights today?" Noelle had black roots and blond tips.

Megan took a step backward, the phrase *still in training* echoing loudly. "I—"

"Let's get you into a chair." Noelle prodded her toward one of the stations.

"You know, I—"

"She's a little nervous. A virgin," Barry said.

Megan's face was suddenly warmed to about a hundred degrees. "That's—"

"Virgin hair," he added, following them. "The rest, I don't know."

Megan clamped her lips together. She was going to get him. How, she didn't know. But sometime in the not-too-distant future, there would be payback.

Before she knew it, Megan was sitting in a chair with Barry behind her as Noelle unpinned her hair and it fell below her shoulders.

"Hey, you've got more hair than I thought." Barry reached out and started gathering up hunks and letting it fall. On her other side, Noelle did the same.

Megan found herself speechless.

"I'm thinking buttery chunks around the face, maybe a little caramel toward the back," Barry suggested.

Was he gay? Megan stared at him in the mirror.

"Men always want to go too blond," Noelle said.

"No, toffee and butterscotch. A little maple sugar for depth."

"How about honey instead of toffee. Right through here." Barry's fingers threaded their way down either side of Megan's face sending tingles to her stomach. Or it could just be hunger.

"Good eye." Noelle nodded as she raked a brush through Megan's hair.

Barry caught Megan's eye in the mirror and made a face. "Don't stare at me like that. I grew up with three sisters! I've spent hours waiting on them in places like this. And I've had way too much experience with weddings lately. A person picks up this kind of stuff."

Megan only sighed. *She* never picked up this kind of stuff.

"Be nice. Be friendly," he said meaningfully. "You'll have plenty of time. Foiling takes a couple of hours."

Lucky for him he was out of kicking range when he said it.

BARRY MADE IT to the Water Oaks Country Club in record time. Unfortunately, he didn't see the van in the parking lot. Great.

Well, he'd wanted a challenge. Now to track down the groomsmen on the golf course.

But luck—which had been a stranger to him lately—revealed two of the groomsmen kicking back in the bar, watching a baseball game on a really fine plasma-screen TV.

"Hey, how's it going?" Barry slid onto the bar stool

nearest them and gestured to the bartender to bring a round of the beers the men were drinking. Lite beer. He hated lite beer. Lite beer, lite men. "We met at the wedding rehearsal. Barry Sutton with the *Press?*"

"Oh, yeah. You're that guy," one of them said.

"I'd like to talk to the groom. Is he around?"

Without taking their eyes from the screen, both men shook their heads.

"Then how about Derek, the best man?"

"Haven't seen him here, either."

Barry was almost tempted to sip at the beer. It was looking as though he was headed out to the golf course after all. "Got any idea about when he might show? Are you two waiting to make a fourth?"

"Nah. We just want to watch the game."

In other words, Barry was the only one who cared about the groom. "You don't actually know the groom and best man, do you?"

Shifting in irritation, one of the guys responded, "We just met him."

"Yeah, they, like, served in the military, or something together."

"And that one dude sure is hyper."

Barry assumed they were referring to the best man. "They didn't get in the limo with you. Did you overhear them say where they were going?"

Both men shook their heads. "They said something about planes. Maybe they're going to pick up somebody at the airport," said one.

"It was a Learjet, dude. Some über-boss is probably flying in."

"Man, you know what those things cost?"

And that was all he was going to get out of them. Checking out of the conversation, Barry slid his untouched beer across their small table and left.

Next up was a fruitless chase in a golf cart. Barry's personal credo in pursuing stories was to tell the truth because then he had less to remember. And then there were the times like these when truth got really stretched. Convincing the attendant, then the course manager, to let him go careening over the course after the golfing groomsmen had required a fair amount of truth stretching along with the use of the word *emergency,* which he preferred not to do, especially when it only resulted in wasting an hour. After all that, Barry got nothing but the impression that no one cared that the groom wasn't golfing with them at all. He returned to the clubhouse.

Sometimes, he reminded himself, a cigar was just a cigar and maybe no one was concerned because there was nothing to be concerned about. Maybe the groom and best man were only picking up someone at the airport. Was he so desperate for a story that he was hallucinating leads?

Except they sure hadn't wanted him to follow them—or maybe that was normal driving. And a normal van.

Right.

He headed for the parking lot toward his car and stopped.

"IF YOU DRY YOUR HAIR upside down, you can get more volume."

Megan stared in the mirror as Noelle put the finishing touches on her hair. How could she get a haircut and end up with *more* hair?

"How is all this going to fit under my uniform hat?"

"You and that hat. I've already told you I left the layers long enough in front for you to pull your hair back. This is for play."

Megan didn't tell Noelle that there wasn't much play in her life. She knew what Noelle meant, but honestly, working the 6:00 a.m. to 3:00 p.m. watch meant early nights. Still, who knew her hair could do this? Her feminine instincts knew this was the kind of hair Barry liked. With a shock, she realized this was the first time she'd had any sort of message from those instincts. Maybe she did have them. Maybe they'd just been asleep. Maybe peroxide woke them up.

"Let's see if Tessa can do your makeup now and then I want a picture for my portfolio."

Well, if she wanted a picture, then that was a good sign. Megan smiled to herself. Tessa was doing the bridesmaids' makeup for tomorrow and had been doing a trial run this afternoon. Megan, showing a talent for subterfuge she hoped impressed Barry, had approached Tessa for advice about how to alter her makeup to go with the lighter hair color and about how it would affect her appearance on camera—assuming she ever got back on camera. All the bridesmaids and the other clients within earshot had weighed in with an opinion and had actually given her some useful tips.

They casually accepted that Megan belonged there. For the first time in her life, Megan had connected with women on a purely feminine level and she liked it.

But she also paid attention to what the wedding party was saying. They were both kind and catty, excited and petulant. In short, normal.

Well, maybe the bride was a little bit over the edge—could her matron of honor help it if she'd gone into labor? Megan stopped herself from asking why the heck Sally hadn't moved up her wedding just to be on the safe side, but it wasn't her place.

And then, there was somebody named Cecily who had a newly prominent role as the maid of honor. An old family friend or something. Anyway, from what Megan gathered, Cecily really needed the spa day, only she wasn't there and the bride was super-miffed.

Megan didn't know if this was the type of information Barry wanted, but this was what she'd learned.

It was all over faster than she'd expected and Megan was looking good, not that she thought she'd looked bad before, but this was a different sort of good. A Barry sort of good.

She was ready to leave and anxious to show off her hair to Barry. He didn't answer his cell phone.

The bridesmaids were finished and watching as Sally's stylist tested the fit of the veil with the upswept hair. "So, how did you and your sweetie meet?" the stylist asked.

Megan edged closer. *She* was supposed to have asked that.

A woman approached. "Would you like a chair massage?"

Megan glanced to her right and saw that in trying to avoid looking as though she were eavesdropping, which she was, she'd wandered next to several oddly shaped chair and bench contraptions.

"Uh…"

"You look tense," the woman said. "Fifteen minutes and you'll melt."

"Okay. Can we go to that one down there?" Megan pointed to the chair closest to Sally.

"…and it got so creepy. It was like that guy was stalking me or something. My dad insisted that we have our home security updated and he hired Gus's company. Dad was even talking bodyguard but once Gus saw me…" Sally gave a self-satisfied grin "…it wasn't necessary, 'cause my body was plenty guarded."

"He's such a hunk," one of her friends said.

Megan didn't know which one because she was busy melting under the ministrations of the masseuse. With her face in the padded cutout, she was probably ruining Tessa's makeup handiwork, but at the moment, she simply didn't care.

Chair massages were heaven and she'd have one every day if she could afford it. Maybe she could, but not here. At least this was Barry's treat today and he was making her wait, so she didn't feel in the least bit guilty. And look what she'd learned. Maybe he'd be so impressed by her hair and her detective skills that he'd offer her dinner. And then…

Megan returned to the reception area and called him from her cell phone. No answer. It was the third time she'd called, and he didn't have his phone turned off…so where was he?

4

BARRY WAS in the Water Oaks Country Club parking lot staring at his car, that's where he was. Specifically, he was staring at the four flat tires on his car. A car that was also missing a crucial part of the engine. What had been attached to those dangling wires? Megan would know.

Was this Gus and Derek's work? Maybe. Maybe not. But Barry had clearly bothered somebody, which meant he was on to something. He stared at his car feeling strangely excited. His reporter's instinct was due for a good workout. It had been too long.

As he punched in Megan's cell phone number, a uniformed man on a golf cart stopped next to his car. Yeah, yeah. So where had all the parking-lot valets been while his car was being vandalized?

"Do you need help, sir?"

Barry shook his head. "I'll just give my auto club a call to come have a look." He chose a vaguely absent smile before turning away so the man would move on. This was not the time to attract attention.

Megan's phone was busy. Busy! When he needed to get through to her. Who could she be talking to?

MEGAN CLOSED her phone. Barry's was busy, but at least she knew he was still alive. She'd already called him an embarrassing number of times.

The bridal party had left and she'd gleaned all the gossip she could—actually, she was rather impressed with herself. She had a knack for getting information, she really did. But now she'd read more women's magazines than she ever had in her life, taken three quizzes and learned that she was not flirting mate-rial—big surprise—and that police uniforms hadn't made the spring fashion hot list.

Where *was* he?

Her phone rang—a plain unadorned ring because her phone wasn't new enough to be able to down-load the cute rings from the Internet—and she forced herself to answer calmly. "Hello?"

"Megan!" Just that. No apology. How was she supposed to respond?

"Barry!" seemed the way to go.

"You're finally off the phone."

"*I'm* off! You're the one burning up all your cell minutes."

There was a brief silence during which Megan re-alized that they'd been calling each other at the same time, and she'd bet Barry was coming to the same conclusion. "So where are you?" she said, rushing on.

"I'm at Water Oaks Country Club. Having a little car trouble—can you come get me?"

Could she—Megan closed her eyes. How typical. If her hair didn't look so good, she'd be angry.

He'd forgotten her. Forgotten that he'd treated her

to a manicure and highlights—and makeup and a chair massage and a deep-conditioning treatment, but he didn't know about all those. In fact, the effects from the chair massage lingered and made it difficult to work up any kind of irritation at all. Luckily for him, she was glass-of-wine mellow.

"Barry, you dropped me off here, remember? I don't have my car."

"That's right." His voice held a forced jauntiness. He was frazzled. Mr. Cool was never frazzled.

Some of her mellowness evaporated. "Are you okay? Were you in an accident?"

"Uh…I'll tell you later."

This didn't sound good. "Barry?"

"So…I need to pick *you* up…"

She could practically hear him thinking. "Don't worry about it. I'll call somebody and come and get you."

"No police," he said quickly.

"And I would be…?"

A beat went by. "Off duty?"

What had he gotten himself into? "Understood," she responded dryly. "Stay there and I'll come rescue you."

"No, no." She could hear a shuffling. "I'll call triple A…if I haven't let my membership lapse. Oh."

Megan suppressed a smile. "I'm coming to get you." And she hung up.

Now, who to call? Gina was off duty and probably going out. It was Friday night. *Megan* should be going out, what with this fabulous hair. Well, she was, wasn't she? She was going out to rescue Barry. It wasn't as though she had anything better to do.

Eventually, Megan had a patrol car in the area drive her the few blocks back to the station parking lot where she retrieved her own car and drove to the country club.

She'd alerted Barry that she was on the way and found him leaning against his car, arms crossed over his chest, laptop at his feet.

He looked really good and Megan admitted to herself that where Barry was concerned, she thought he looked good all the time. Wasn't admitting your weakness the first step in overcoming it? So, Barry looked good. She'd admit it and empower herself.

But she still didn't feel any progress toward overcoming her weakness.

Unsmiling, he watched her drive toward him. Maybe he didn't recognize her. Oh, right. This was the new serious look he'd chosen for her.

She forgot about his calculated expressions when she saw the flat tires on his car. Barry crooked his finger as she drove up beside him. "All four?" she asked.

Barry nodded.

One flat tire could have been an accident. Even two, if he'd driven over something, but four? Four was a message.

Who'd want to send Barry a message? Well, she did, but it wasn't a flat-tire kind of message.

As Megan got out of her car, Barry opened the hood of his car and pointed. "What's missing here?"

Megan glanced at the dangling wires. "Distributor cap."

He dropped the hood. "At least parts for old Mustangs aren't that hard to find, but they do take some effort." He glanced at her. "And time."

"Yeah, well, if you're planning to put it on yourself, make sure you get the cables plugged back in the right order."

"Oh, great," he muttered.

They got into Megan's car without Barry mentioning her hair.

Megan started her car—a reliable but older Honda Civic, which had all its parts—and twisted her head around as she backed up. Still no comment from Barry and she'd practically whipped him in the face with her hair.

"Where can I drop you off?" Megan was hungry and she held out a slim hope that he'd offer her dinner. She wasn't dressed for any place fancy, so it wouldn't be a big deal. Just nice and easy. Was that asking too much?

"I need another favor," he said. "I'd like to go back to the station so we can check out Sterling International some more."

Oh, that was just *it*. Megan skidded on the gravel as she stopped the car right in front of the guard gate. Whipping her hair around—*take that, Barry*—she glared at him.

"What?"

"I am not a doormat. Do I look as though I've got 'welcome' stamped across my forehead?"

BEFORE HE COULD STOP himself, Barry glanced at her forehead. Her eyes narrowed.

What had he done? "What's the matter? Why aren't you driving?"

"I'm tired of you taking advantage of me."

For the love of— "I'm doing you a favor! There's possible criminal activity going on here. I'm offering you the tip. You'll get brownie points."

"Right."

He hadn't really expected that to work. Barry switched tactics. "Come on, Megan." He spoke in a you-know-you-want-to voice. "I'm only asking for ten minutes with your database. I'm on to something. I know it. You know it."

Megan exhaled heavily and stared out the windshield. Good. She was weakening. "Barry…"

"I mean, you don't have anything else going on, do you?"

She closed her eyes. "Get out."

"What?"

"You heard me. Get out of the car."

Why was Megan picking now to become difficult? She used to be so sweet. Barry studied her, trying to figure out the best approach to get her to do what he wanted.

And suddenly he noticed her hair. Late afternoon sun glinted off golden, shoulder-length waves. He stared and stared some more. Wow. Double wow. Off the chart wow.

How could he have missed that hair? Megan had definitely gone over to the light side. She looked… hot. Incandescently hot.

And the way she glared at him—an angry almost-blonde—made him feel hot, too. Awareness swept through him, dragging desire right behind it. He'd always thought Megan had potential and knew he wasn't the only one. A huge part of her appeal was that the men who saw her fantasized about liberating the sexy potential of the earnest police spokeswoman with the well-filled uniform.

And now, here she was. Liberated.

The underlying zing was now front and center. "You…look…fantastic." He felt as though he were talking through a mouthful of molasses.

She blinked, but otherwise, her expression didn't change.

He should have tossed off some casual, "Hey, lookin' good, kid," remark. Too late now. "Your hair—" he gestured "—came out well." Did his voice crack?

"Came out well? After two and a half hours, I'd hoped for more than 'came out well.'"

What did she want him to say? He couldn't read her. All that newly blond hair had fuzzed his reception. "Megan…I already told you that you look fantastic. The truth is, you look hot. I wasn't sure I should mention that. Okay?"

She smiled slightly. "Okay."

He hadn't sold it yet. "I mean it. You look really, really good." But that sounded as though he hadn't thought she looked good before. "Not that you didn't always look good, but it was good in a different way. A less hot…way." Boy, that was slick. "And…and it's an appropriate way…for your job. And now…"

She raised a newly shaped eyebrow and he felt the impact hit right below the belt. "I look inappropriate?"

Complimenting women was his specialty. What had happened to him? "In my book, looking hot is never inappropriate."

Rolling her eyes, Megan took her foot off the brake. "Barry, you are so full of it. No wonder your initials are B.S."

She had no idea how good she looked. He stared at her some more, taking in the way her lightened hair enhanced her skin, noticed the new makeup, and the short, no-nonsense, but nicely shaped and buffed nails on the hands that gripped the steering wheel. He imagined those same hands gripping a gun as she tossed that hair and stared down some perp. Holy—

Okay. Time to focus, and not on Megan. Right. Focus. Why couldn't he focus?

Barry dragged his gaze away from Megan and concentrated on keeping it straight ahead. They'd left the gates of the country club and were tooling along the highway. "Where are we going?"

"Back to the station so you can use the database."

They were? If ever there was a case of snatching victory from the jaws of defeat, this was it and he didn't even know how he'd done it.

HE THOUGHT she was hot. Barry Sutton thought she was hot. He'd told her and she believed him. And that was the *only* reason Megan had given in to Barry yet again. And if she wanted to do a favor for a guy who thought she was hot, then why shouldn't she? No need to feel guilty. Lots of women were flattered into doing a lot more than taking a civilian into a police station and allowing him information from Department Only files. Megan planned to sit right next to him and do the searching herself, so it wasn't as though she planned to give *him* access. And she didn't have to tell him anything she didn't want to.

It might be considered slightly stretching the rules, but they *were* supposed to be security-conscious about the wedding and the VIP guests and if Barry *had* stumbled across something…

Amazing how she could rationalize letting Barry get his own way. She knew what he was doing and he was *still* able to manipulate her.

Personally, if she weren't under his influence, she would admit that he was really exaggerating the importance of the groom's disappearance. She should point that out. "Barry, you do realize that the groom is probably attending to last-minute honeymoon details or picking up a gift or driving relatives from the airport or just plain taking a nap?"

"Oh, taking a nap. Hadn't thought of that." Barry opened his laptop. "Lemme just tell you what I've found out so far about one Augustus Hargrove and friend."

By the time they got back to the police station and Megan had heard the story of the whitewashed backgrounds, the security company, the steely eyed stares, the white van and the evasive driving, she didn't feel Barry was exaggerating quite so much.

Half an hour later, after they'd discovered that Augustus Hargrove used to work for Sterling International, she wondered if she should bring in a detective.

"Not yet," Barry said.

They were staring at another conspiracy theory Web site. Normally, not the place to go for rational and accurate information. But it was the only place they'd found anything significant about Sterling International.

"Are you sure that's the one?" Megan asked for the third time.

"It says it's a front for a stealth organization exclusively for the use of Congress."

"I can read."

"It says it's basically a group of military-trained enforcers."

"I told you, I can read. And I don't believe everything I read, especially on these Web sites."

Barry gazed intently into her eyes. She wished he wouldn't do that. "Megan, we haven't found squat about Sterling. Lots of dead ends. This is the only place that even hints at what it might be."

He had such gorgeous blue eyes. Blue, blue, blue.

"I'm one hundred percent positive that Sterling International is a government front."

His chin was...perfect. Wonderfully shaped with a hint of dimple. Not too jutting, in no way receding. Complementing the jaw. Manly. Yes. That was it. Manly, manly, manly.

"I think Congressman Galloway is involved," Barry continued. "He's here making a nice hometown grandstand by attending the wedding and all of a sudden we have a stealth government surveillance van driving around."

His voice was a tenor with husky edges and currently held just that right amount of conviction. A man who had convictions was sexy, she found. Sexy, sexy, sexy.

He pulled his chair right next to hers. She inhaled deeply.

"See what you can find out about Gus and Derek and Sterling in the police files." His gaze was fixed firmly on the computer monitor.

Intensity and single-mindedness was also sexy. It even smelled sexy.

"Megan?" His head turned.

"Hmm?" She met his eyes.

"The files? Or better yet, just bring up whatever the heck you can find about Derek Stafford."

He'd leaned closer to her, so close that she could see the beginning of a sexy stubble shading that perfect chin and manly jaw.

"Here." He reached across her chest and Megan gritted her teeth, half hoping he'd brush against her and half dreading that he would. "I'll just type in—"

"No!" Watching Barry enter her password—the rat had watched her type it—snapped Megan out of her trance. "I can't believe you figured out my password," she grumbled.

He shrugged it off and continued to type. "I'm very observant."

"And I'm very mad."

He sucked in his breath between his teeth. "Megan, we don't have a whole lot of time here."

She powered down her computer. "We're *done* here."

"Megan, please."

The eyes, the chin, the voice, the intensity…it was too much. As Megan opened her drawer so the index cards were visible, she reflected that she wanted Barry begging, but not like this. "I'm not invading the privacy of a citizen without due cause."

"I'm trying to prevent due cause! Due cause might be death or disaster!" He'd raised his voice, but then he'd had to because there was some noisy commotion going on near the dispatcher's desk.

Two detectives left on the run.

"What's going on?" Barry asked.

Megan wished she hadn't turned off her computer. She really wished Barry hadn't jumped up and yelled, "What's up?" across the squad room.

A sergeant Megan had never liked sneered in Barry's direction. "Nothing you need to worry about, society boy. Too bad, too, 'cause you'd be first media at the scene."

"What scene?" Barry snapped.

"Break-in at the Courtland Hotel," someone else answered. "Congressman Galloway's room."

Barry froze. As for Megan, she just felt the familiar queasiness she always felt when she heard Congressman Galloway's name these days.

But instead of heading out the door, Barry turned and sat down. Staring her right in the eyes, he said, "Sounds like due cause to me."

"You think there's a connection?"

"We were both busted for divulging too much information about Galloway and his supposed cooperation in a bribery sting. The investigation was blown, so he's out of it, right? Except here he is, a guest at the wedding of his good friend's daughter. On the surface, so what? Except we've got a groom and best man with covert government pasts who are acting, well, covert. We have a break-in. Don't you think there's a connection?"

"Well, kinda sorta. Maybe." She didn't want there to be a connection. She never wanted to see, hear or vote for the congressman ever again.

"Let's go." Barry grabbed her hand.

Megan was caught off guard by the physical contact. Barry was holding her hand! Barry was holding her hand!

"Go where?" she asked as they stood.

He looked at her in surprise. "To the hotel."

He was holding her hand and he wanted her, Megan Esterbrook, to go with him to the hotel. Happiness welled up within Megan until she remembered that she was the one with the car.

Megan slithered her hand from his grasp. "Okay."

Going to the congressman's hotel was the last thing she wanted to do, but she knew Barry was going anyway and she had a duty to see that he didn't break any laws while doing whatever he was going to do.

"You're the best, Megan." And there was that smile. When would she ever get a real, uncalculated one? "Yeah, I know." She reached over to shut her drawer and at the last minute grabbed the index cards. She had a feeling she was going to need them.

They arrived at the hotel and when Megan saw the yellow crime-scene tape, she knew what Barry was going to ask before he asked it.

And sure enough. "Why are we stopped? Just flash your badge and get us past that stuff."

Megan shook her head. "You are nonessential personnel—"

"I'm a member of the press. The Constitution thinks I'm very essential."

Megan smiled. "Fine." She indicated the group of police officers controlling the growing crowd outside the entrance to the hotel. "Go for it."

"Megan…"

"I'm not on duty and even if I were, I wouldn't be at this scene. I'm public relations."

He pointed to the crowd. "There's the public. Go relate."

Why had she brought him here?

"At least find out what was taken. Come on. Get me something to call in."

"Stay here." Megan got out of the car only because she knew he'd badger her until she did. Learning anything would be tricky, though.

Stepping to the edge of the tape, she approached an officer she recognized. "Hey, Gordy, what's up?"

"Whoa, Megan. Heard about the hair. Nice."

Did she look *that* different? "Thanks, but what can you tell me about this?"

Gordy's face took on a remote look. "I hadn't heard you were the mouth again."

"I'm not." She decided to confess, "Barry Sutton is here looking for a scoop."

Gordy was silent and Megan knew he was thinking about their ill-fated connection to Congressman

Galloway. "Sorry, Megan." There might have been pity in his voice, but Megan hoped not.

"It was worth a shot." Her smile was as fake as any of Barry's. "But more press is only minutes away. Some free advice—figure out what you're going to say before a microphone gets shoved in your face."

When Megan reached the edge of the crowd, a hand grasped her arm. Barry had not waited in the car. "That's it? You're giving up?"

Megan was very aware of Barry's touch through the fleece of her hoodie. Kind of a sexy/unsexy mix and she was the unsexy half. But—she suppressed a sigh—Barry provided enough sexiness for both of them. "They aren't going to tell me—or you—anything."

"What have they got against me?"

Megan gave him a look.

He grimaced. "Oh, yeah, that."

"I can't believe you've forgotten 'that.'"

He slipped his hand around to the small of her back and guided her protectively through the curious onlookers toward the hotel garage. She should have been protecting *him,* but she enjoyed the courtesy.

"I haven't forgotten, but I don't dwell on it." He glanced down at her. "You know, if we do find that the congressman is—"

"Don't go there."

"I *should* go there. Somebody needs to go there. He's completely snowed you people."

"Barry…" Megan trailed off when he opened the door to the stairwell. "Where are we going?"

"To the walkway. Less crowded up there."

Megan stopped. "You know uniforms will be stationed up there, as well."

Barry nudged her forward. "It was a break-in, not a murder. Does the Dallas PD really have that much spare man—person-power on a Friday night?"

"No."

"Then, come on."

"I mean, no, I'm not coming with you."

"Megan." He spoke in a mock-scolding tone that should have irritated her, but didn't. "I need you to run interference. Maybe create a tiny, little distraction."

He was incorrigible. And yet…somehow she was allowing herself to be cajoled up the first flight of stairs.

It was his hand on the small of her back, that's what it was. She shouldn't let him touch her. Running up the last couple of steps to the landing, Megan got her cards out of her purse and read the top one. Okay, right. Good. That was more like it. "Barry, here's where we part," she told him calmly and started back down the stairs. "I'm not interfering in an active police investigation for you. You do whatever you're going to do. I'm going home."

WHAT HAPPENED? Barry allowed her to get all the way to the bottom of the stairs before calling out to her. She kept going.

He was losing his touch with her. Come to think of it, was it just with Megan or was he losing his touch in general?

He caught up with her as she was pulling open the

glass door to the parking garage only because she'd stopped to stuff something in her purse.

"What have you got there?"

"Nothing." She wouldn't meet his eyes.

Barry grabbed and came up with a handful of index cards.

"Give those back!"

"In a minute." He flipped through them and saw his name a couple of times. "What are these?" He held them up in front of her face. She reached out, but he raised his arm.

Megan gazed at him coolly, a look he didn't remember seeing on her face before—or was it the hair's influence? Either way, she wasn't a happy camper.

"You are a bad influence on me."

This required his Harrison Ford/Indiana Jones smile. "Some people might think that's a good thing."

She must not have been an Indiana Jones fan. "Well, it gets me into trouble. Only when I'm around you, I forget that it gets me into trouble. Thus, the Barry aversion therapy was born. On each one of those cards is an incident when you either used me, took advantage of me, let me down, betrayed me, ignored me, forgot about me, inconvenienced me, tricked me, embarrassed me, got me in trouble, mocked me, or just plain irritated the heck out of me."

She plucked the cards from his unresisting grasp. "When I feel myself being unduly influenced by your...your...*you*, I read the cards and strengthen my resolve."

Barry was totally taken aback. He'd never been

faced with anyone who resented him before. To be honest, he never felt he'd done serious harm to anyone. Ever. Outmaneuvered someone, sure, but that was just business.

"You just described a horrible person. I am not a horrible person. I'm a nice guy." He pointed to his chest for emphasis. "I make it a point to be a nice guy. People like nice guys. Everyone likes me. Therefore, I'm a nice guy."

Megan met his eyes. "Okay, nice guy, listen to this." Then she read aloud from one of the cards. "Barry Sutton promised to be available to answer questions for an elementary-school tour of the newspaper."

Barry went blank. What was she talking about? "What tour?"

"It was last year," Megan prompted. "I asked you on behalf of a teacher friend of mine. Since I'd done you so many favors, I figured you wouldn't object. And you didn't. At least at the time. At the time, you promised all kinds of things."

A vague memory stirred.

"But the day of the tour, you weren't there."

"I remember now. I'm sorry, but crime doesn't wait for school tours. I was on assignment."

"Then you should have arranged for someone to take your place."

He should have. "You're right. I should have. I'm sorry."

Megan nodded.

"Hey, why don't I go visit the class personally and talk to them about working for a newspaper?"

"It's a different class now."

"Oh. Same teacher?"

"You don't have to—"

"I want to make it up to her. To you." He patted his pockets for his pen. "What's her name?" He took the index card from Megan and flipped it over.

She looked so skeptical, his pride was stung. "I will call her," he reiterated. "Let me do this."

"Elisha Tenny at Morning West Elementary."

"Got it." He folded the card and put it and the pen in his pocket, a little shocked at how many cards Megan was left holding. "And we're going to get to the rest of those, too."

Megan stuck them in her purse. "It'll take a while."

He looked her square in the eyes. "Have I really been that bad to you?"

"Only because I let you."

She must hate him and he couldn't stand the thought of her hating him. "Megan—"

She stopped him with a shake of her head and a sigh. "Let's go see what we can find out about the break-in. You have as much right to be there as anyone."

5

THEY WORKED THEIR WAY to the sixth floor where it was no problem at all to locate the congressman's suite. First, there was the yellow tape, and second, there were police crowding the hallway.

Barry gave a low whistle. "Quite a response for a simple break-in."

That's what Megan thought. "Maybe they're trying to make it up to Congressman Galloway since we blew the investigation last year." She felt him glance down at her.

"You haven't ever taken a course in building esteem, have you?"

"Barry, it happened. On your side, maybe it wasn't such a big deal, but on my side..." She didn't finish because she didn't want to reveal just how bad it had really been for her and because he was, after all, a member of the press. She wasn't the current official spokeswoman, but that didn't mean she wouldn't be quoted. This was Barry, she reminded herself. Nothing was off the record with him.

"I can go talk to the detectives for you," she offered.

"Not this time." He withdrew a small digital recorder. "I'll talk to them myself."

Megan tagged along as Barry questioned various officers. To her surprise, he asked mostly the same questions. Even more surprising, he received different pieces of information, which gave him a larger picture than she knew the department would want him to have. And he made it look easy.

What an eye-opener. Megan now understood what had happened seven months ago. She'd said one thing and clearly others had added to the official statements. All Barry had done was connect the dots.

Knowing this made her feel marginally better. In the future, when the department made statements, they needed to make sure that they were all revealing and concealing the same information. Also, only official spokespeople should be talking to the press. And as soon as she got into work on Monday, she was sending a memo to that effect. Seven months of her life and maybe a permanent career-altering detour—and it wasn't even her fault.

And neither was it Barry's fault. He was just very, very good at what he did. Megan exhaled, releasing a weight she'd carried for months. She'd never hated Barry the way she'd felt he deserved and was relieved she didn't have to manufacture emotions she didn't truly feel. *However,* and that was a very big however, he was still slick, and he could still get her into trouble and she still had to watch what she said to him.

Oh, yeah. And she still wanted to spend private time with him on the nearest horizontal surface. Barry drew her down the hall to a small bench by the elevators. Horizontal, yes, private, no. Pity.

Megan silently watched as he put in an earpiece and replayed the information he'd collected. His long fingers scribbled with a pencil in a tiny spiral notebook. She smiled at the incongruity of the old-fashioned pencil and paper and the high-tech recording device. A mix of old and new. Was that an insight into the real Barry?

She had such a thing for him, but realistically, what would she do if he responded?

Barry as a boyfriend? She tested the relationship in her mind. Aside from the obvious, what would she do with him? Would she ever be able to fully trust him? No. Would she ever fully relax around him? No. Would she even be able to hold his interest for any length of time? Sadly, no. Would she have fun trying?

You betcha.

She sighed.

What kind of woman would Barry go for? He could pretty much have his pick, but Megan couldn't see him with a high-maintenance type, unless she was self-maintaining.

Or maybe he'd like that type. He certainly knew his way around a salon. He did say he'd grown up with sisters. Megan got the idea that they were girlie girls and not the tomboy type she was. She kept trying to tap into her inner femininity, but it would never feel natural to her.

She caught sight of herself in the mirror next to the elevator and touched her hair. It looked so glamorous, and what was she wearing? A hooded sweatshirt over an undershirt and jeans. The hair required better than that. Maybe the trick was in the details. Lots and lots of time-consuming details.

"Okay." Barry pulled out the earpiece and stuffed it into his pocket. "Here's the deal. No official word on what was taken. That doesn't mean that something wasn't taken, but we're not going to be told. We do know that the place was tossed—and tossed pretty good. Not in the usual looking-for-something way, but in the trash-it way. Clothes were everywhere. And apparently the congressman's sister is due in because her suitcase was emptied, too. They're waiting to contact her to see if anything is missing."

"You got all that?" Megan asked. Even though she'd listened to him, she'd missed details. It was an eye-opener.

"There's more. The consensus is that this was a professional job. We know the groom and his buddy are a couple of pros involved with a shadowy security organization that serves congress. Congressman Galloway's room was burgled. Therefore—"

"Stretching, stretching."

"Therefore," Barry continued, "I figure one of three things has happened." He ticked them off with his fingers. "Either the congressman called Gus and Derek before his wife reported the break-in and they're doing their own investigation, or dear old Congressman Galloway truly is being blackmailed and one of them, say Gus, stole incriminating evidence, or the wedding is a cover to pass information to somebody, or the whole thing is just a coincidence."

"That's four things."

"Hey, I figure you know more about last year's investigation than I do." He tugged on a strand of her hair. "I'm hoping you'll work with me here."

Megan was torn between being flattered and knowing she'd regret getting involved.

Barry gave her a considering look. "You know, last year you were just doing your job. You got stomped on pretty good. Did you ever wonder why?"

Only every hour of every day since then.

Barry gazed at the crowd of police. "Now me, I made a couple of lucky guesses without getting the facts verified the way I should have. It was appropriate for me to have been reprimanded. But reassigned for this long?" He shook his head. "Sounds to me as though somebody got to somebody and we both suffered because of it."

Megan tried to cut through all the Barry slickness and evaluate the merits of his theory. She wanted to believe him, but should she?

"Wouldn't you like the chance to catch them on it? Wouldn't you like vindication?" He very cleverly appealed to her professional pride.

"Investigating really isn't my thing," she told him.

"But it's mine." He leaned forward, invading her personal space. "Work with me."

Part of her immediately responded to his blue, blue eyes with the appealing crinkles, and the other part was jumping up and down wildly pointing out that he was only looking for a chauffeur.

She clutched her purse trying to feel the cards inside. What should she do? Read a card. That's why she brought them. She fumbled with the zipper on her purse.

"Tell you what." He backed up and flipped through the pages in his notebook. "Here's the van's plate." He showed it to her. "Humor me and call it in. See if it's shown up somewhere between Water Oaks Country Club and the airport."

The stupid zipper on her purse was stuck. Megan spoke carefully. "Barry, Dallas is a very large city and—"

He waved away her words. "You and I both know there are cameras recording license plates all over the city. You don't have to admit it, just tap into it. I won't even listen." He stuck his fingers in his ears.

Oh, why not? Megan moved down the hall away from Barry. Within minutes, the airport security system at Love Field confirmed that a van bearing that license number had entered one of the terminal parking areas.

Megan looked over at Barry and felt a little tug. Make that a really big tug. The kind of tug that got a girl into trouble. The kind of tug that resulted in a trip to the airport.

BEFORE MAKING Megan drive all the way to Love Field, Barry made a couple of quick phone calls. As he'd suspected, the rehearsal dinner was about to start, but neither the groom nor the best man was there, and better yet, no one knew where they were.

He flipped his cell phone shut. "In other words, if he's picking up a guest, nobody knows about it."

"So what's going on?" Megan asked.

"We're going to find out what's going on." Barry glanced over at her and got a little zing. He kept forgetting her changed appearance. The zinging was so very nice and so was the way she looked right now. He was going to have to watch himself. "You, uh, aren't averse to showing your badge around, are you?"

"I would prefer not to."

A vision of Megan with her hair down and wavy and blond and, um, bearing no small resemblance to fantasy comic-book heroines popped into his mind. He was pretty sure she had the requisite fantasy equipment underneath that sweatshirt. "Have you got your gun?" And that was not the fantasy equipment foremost in his mind.

"No!"

That was a short-lived fantasy, though the gun was only part of it.

She lowered her voice. "I'm not a street cop."

"I've seen you with your gun before." He glanced at her. "You look good with a gun." Understatement, understatement. And oh, so very inappropriate.

"Barry, it's not an accessory." She hoisted her purse over her shoulder. "If we're going to the airport, then let's get going. Though how you expect to find anything or anyone sure beats me. What do you plan to do? Run around the terminals and hope we catch the groom waiting in line somewhere? And if, by some miracle, you do find him, what are you going to do with him?"

They were back on the walkway, which arched over a busy downtown street, when Megan asked her very excellent questions. It was his job to come up with some very excellent answers.

He should be at the rehearsal dinner. His editor

would want a write-up—the food, the clothes, the wines. Although it was unlikely that anything about the dinner would be published in connection with the wedding, Barry knew the information would appear in a future article featuring restaurants or something. Whatever. Right now, Barry didn't care. He'd interview somebody afterward. Or maybe while Megan was driving him to the airport. Yeah. That's what he'd do.

"Barry? Do you have a plan?"

"Sort of." Hadn't he just come up with the plan to go to the airport? How many plans was he supposed to generate in sixty seconds?

"Barry?" A few minutes had passed, and they were approaching her car.

He'd say one thing, she wasn't a babbler. "I'm thinking."

"Think out loud."

"Okay. Where would this guy go? I'm thinking Washington, D.C."

"Out of nowhere you come up with this? Why?"

"It fits. I'm also thinking he hadn't planned to, since he doesn't have a good cover for missing the rehearsal dinner."

"You don't know that he's missing it."

"He wasn't there when I called and the van is at the airport. So…I can start checking airlines—we caught a break that he's at Love Field and not Dallas/Fort Worth so we're only dealing with Southwest and a couple of small commuter lines and Southwest doesn't fly into…a plane!" Barry grinned at Megan in triumph. "The groomsmen mentioned that they heard Gus and Derek talking about planes. Five bucks says he's got his own plane." And in only two phone calls, Barry confirmed that Gus's security company owned a plane hangared at Love Field. "It's at an FBO—fixed base operator—called Corporate Jet Service. And it hasn't been cleared for takeoff yet. Let's go."

Megan hadn't popped the locks on her car. In fact, she was just standing there staring at him.

"Come on." He gestured to the door.

"You...the way you do that? Put pieces together? It's scary."

"Thanks. Open the door."

WITH ALL THE HEIGHTENED security these days, Megan was appalled at how easy it was to make their way to the hangar housing the Hargrove Security Systems corporate jet.

As they walked up to the entryway, she noted the area was eerily deserted. The Corporate Jet Service building was some distance away. A small plane must have recently arrived and was parked under the canopy. Lights shone from the lobby of the building, which made this area seem darker.

The newly blond hair on the back of Megan's neck stood up. Barry had reporter's instinct; she had cop's instinct. Or more accurately, unarmed-woman-in-a-dark-airplane-hangar-at-dusk instincts. The other plane, an impressive Learjet, had been pulled out, but no one was in the area, and that was weird. Had it already been serviced?

"Barry?" she whispered.

He held up his hand in the universal gesture for quiet.

Well, duh.

Megan stepped to one side in hopes that he would follow her. They'd been silhouetted in the doorway against the unlit interior. Very bad sneaking-around strategy. But no. Barry tromped on inside, leaving her a fair distance behind. Okay, not tromped, but not exactly moving quietly. She could hear him fumbling against the walls, presumably looking for the light switch. What an idiot! And she'd thought he was smart!

Which was why she was totally taken off guard when a hand covered her mouth and an arm locked her neck in a position that made any of her defense moves impossible. Even as the adrenaline spurted through her, she recognized that this guy knew what he was doing. She went completely still.

"Smart girl," he whispered in her ear.

Oh, so very smart. That's why I was caught off guard.

"I don't intend to hurt you, but you know I can."

"Uh-huh," she sounded against his hand.

Fortunately, it was a clean hand. She noted that he didn't smoke, had recently bathed, and his clothing held a whiff of dry-cleaning solvent. His voice had the accentless delivery of a newscaster and he gave the impression of intelligence. A pro. Maybe government, maybe not, though she was held in the same grip she'd been taught—the one a person never wanted to be in.

"Now, if your boyfriend would hurry up and find the lights—"

"Nah i oyend!"

"Not your boyfriend?" Megan heard a soft chuckle. "Whatever, sweetheart."

Actually, knowing she was in the hands of a professional softened her involuntary panic. Amateurs made mistakes. Professionals stayed focused and as long as you weren't their focus, you had a pretty good chance of staying alive.

Which naturally begged the question of who exactly was this professional's focus.

Fluorescent light suddenly spilled from the open hangar.

"Hey, Megan!" Barry called. "Where are you? Afraid of the dark?"

Briefly, Megan toyed with the idea of making noise or making her body go suddenly limp. As though he could read her mind, the man holding her twisted her neck ever so slightly. All right, already. He could snap her neck. She got the message.

"Megan?"

Pro though he was, there was going to be a moment when her captor's attention was divided, and judging by Barry's echoing footsteps, that moment was at hand.

Megan braced herself to take advantage if the guy loosened his grip.

Barry's shadow appeared first and Megan's captor immediately tilted her off balance so she had to cling to his arm or lose consciousness.

The man was good, and strong—he raised a small handgun—and armed.

"Megan?" Barry came into view, throwing up his hands as soon as he saw them. "Oh, hey! It's you."

Barry dropped his hands and continued walking toward them. "Megan, you found our missing groom. Good job."

HIS VOICE STILL WORKED. Considering Barry's heart was in his throat, he was grateful.

Megan was clinging to Gus's arm, her neck at an unnatural angle, that new hair of hers tangled around his wrist. She looked super-pissed and a little embarrassed, but not scared.

Knowing Megan was okay meant Barry could concentrate on Gus and figure a way to talk them out of this.

His gut impression was that Gus was not a threat. Oh, sure, there was the gun and all, but Barry ignored that.

"I prefer your feet and hands where they were," Gus said.

"Hey, we're no threat." Barry stopped walking, but he didn't back up. "Barry Sutton." He stuck out his hand. "I'm covering your wedding for the *Dallas Press*. You're a hard man to track down."

"I know who you are."

Gus didn't shake his hand, but Barry hadn't expected him to. "Got a couple of questions for you." He reached into his pocket for his recorder. "You can put away the piece and let Megan go."

"Freeze."

Barry froze, but he wasn't happy about it. Gus the groom could have taken the easy way out Barry offered, but no, he was going to play this whole thing out. "It's a recorder." Barry dropped all affability from his voice. "I'm not exactly Quick Draw Mc-Graw." He nodded to Megan. "Let her go. Now."

Gus smiled faintly. "You're in no position to give orders."

"Oh, please. You're not going to shoot us." He hoped. He really, really, hoped. "You just want to scare us so we'll leave you alone to do whatever it is you're doing."

A beat went by while Gus took his measure. "Is it working?"

"Eh." Barry shrugged.

"Yeah, blondie here doesn't seem overwhelmed with panic, either." Amiable though he sounded, Gus still hadn't lowered the gun. Important point, that.

"May I unfreeze?" Barry asked.

"Take the recorder and toss it on the floor. Nice and easy."

"I'll slowly remove the recorder and place it gently on the floor thus preserving my notes on the floral arrangements for your wedding. You remember your wedding? The one that's tomorrow?" Barry hoped that by emphasizing the wedding, Gus wouldn't guess that they knew anything more.

"I remember. So you understand my tight schedule and how I can't spend any more time chitchatting with you two."

"*Eht ee go!*"

"I will let you go," Gus said calmly. "And you will walk over to join your boyfriend—"

"*Nah i oyend!*"

"—your not-boyfriend, and in doing so you will not make any untoward moves—I'm assuming I don't need to define untoward moves—or I will shoot you in a noncritical body part."

Though he spoke casually, the man was serious and clearly didn't fall for Barry's we're-just-clueless-bystanders performance. Rats.

"Sounds reasonable," Barry said. "Doesn't that sound reasonable, Megan? And I'll just speak for the both of us when I say that we consider all our body parts critical, so there won't be any untoward moves, will there, Megan?" Barry spoke as sternly as he dared to her. It was tricky because he didn't want her to rebel against the tone he used and he sure didn't want her doing anything stupid.

Megan grunted something that sounded like, "Okay." At least it wasn't something stupid like, "You're under arrest." He didn't know if Gus knew Megan was a police officer and he didn't see the advantage in him finding out.

Gus released his hold on Megan, but kept his eyes on Barry as though he were the real threat. He felt a masculine pride, which was completely inappropriate, given the circumstances.

Megan glared at Gus as she massaged her neck.

Barry's gaze got tangled up in her unconsciously sensual movements—also completely inappropriate.

"The purse, blondie," Gus said.

Megan seemed to ignore him as she took in Barry watching her.

Not good. "Megan? The man with the gun is speaking to you."

She looked startled and then her lips curled in a

tiny smile as she touched her hair. It was gone by the time she flung her purse at Gus.

But Barry considered that smile. That smile—call it an awakening of feminine power—made his mouth go dry.

Megan stood next to him and he gave her arm a reassuring squeeze. Okay, it was an excuse to touch her. Barry knew he was in bad shape when the fact that a man holding a gun on them was overshadowed by his need to have Megan within touching distance.

"You okay?" he asked softly, then cleared his throat so he could assume a more matter-of-fact tone.

"I'm fine." She shot a look at their errant groom. "But my neck is sore."

Barry stopped himself from offering a neck rub and reminded himself that they weren't in a neck-rub situation.

He faced Gus and saw him studying them.

With a smile very like the one on Megan's face a few minutes ago, he squatted and upended her purse. He still managed to keep the gun on them, a skill Barry thought he might more fully appreciate another time.

After glancing at the cascaded stack of index cards, Gus gave both of them another long look and then poked through a pile that didn't resemble the contents of any purse Barry's sisters carried. Where were the tubes and mirrors and the half-dozen lipsticks? Other than a couple of tissues that had seen better days and a brush, it might have been a guy's purse—if a guy carried a purse.

"Huh." Gus nudged a black folded wallet. "I

know what this is." He repositioned the gun so it was more toward Megan. "So it's Officer Blondie."

Barry took a protective step closer to her, which fed some private amusement of Gus's.

"Where's your service revolver, Officer Blondie?"

"It's Megan. I'm off duty."

"Where's your off-duty weapon?"

"I'm not carrying."

Gus raised his eyebrows.

"I'm in media relations," Megan explained with a glance toward Barry. "You know the press. Having a gun handy would just be too tempting."

Barry ignored the crack. "She's not here as the police. I had car trouble."

"So what are you doing here, Not-boyfriend?"

"Looking for you," Barry answered. Why lie?

"You're very resourceful." He studied the two of them again, his gaze flicking back and forth.

"So what's up?" Barry asked. "Anything to do with Congressman Galloway? Anything to do with the congressman's hotel room?"

Gus put everything back into Megan's purse except her cell phone and stood. "As I said, I've got things to do and you two are slowing me down."

"How about a hint?" Barry asked.

Megan jabbed him with her elbow.

"Megan, I've got to ask. What's the worst that could happen?" he reasoned in full hearing of Gus.

"He could shoot us."

"I'm talking other than that. All he can say is 'no.' Hey, Gus, I was investigating Congressman Galloway and got crossways with an ongoing police case.

I figure he's taking a stroll on the shady side of the street. Am I right?"

"What makes you think I have any idea?" Holding his arm out, Gus checked his watch without breaking the stare he kept fixed on them.

Nice trick. Barry might just practice that one. "We're way past denials, here."

"I'm a good guy—that's all you need to know. But I'm still going to tie you up." He gestured toward a workbench in the maintenance area to the rear of the hangar.

"You're tying us up?" Megan started walking. "Oh, what fun. Just the way I wanted to spend my Friday night."

Megan sarcastic? Determinedly diplomatic Megan?

"It can be," Gus murmured.

Barry didn't like the sound of that. "I'm pretty sure this is illegal. Megan'll back me up."

Megan remained significantly silent.

"Megan?" Barry prompted.

"Oh, I can eventually get him arrested, but I can guarantee that he's one of those guys who'll be released within the hour after the captain gets a phone call and some sealed orders. Am I right, Gus?"

Gus smiled blandly. "On the floor."

"I'm right." Sighing loudly, Megan sank to the gritty concrete floor and crossed her wrists behind her. This naturally pulled apart her hoodie and strained her T-shirt across her chest.

"You're getting married tomorrow," Barry reminded him.

"On the floor," Gus ordered.

Barry sat next to Megan while Gus rummaged on the workbench. "Tie wraps. The restraining device of choice."

"Nuts." Megan didn't look happy.

When Barry looked a question at her she explained. "Police use them."

"Face each other. Megan, scoot yourself between Not-boyfriend's legs."

"*What?*"

"Do it." He looked at Barry. "Spread 'em."

Barry gave him a cold look and moved his legs apart. Under Gus's direction, Megan slid between them.

"Legs around his waist."

"Hey!" Barry stared at Megan, whose face was curiously blank as she gripped her legs around his waist. From the movements behind him, he figured Gus was tying her ankles together.

Barry didn't like this. All right, he did, but he really didn't want to.

He felt Gus cross his wrists behind his back and heard the zipper sound as the tie wrap closed around them.

"You can thank me later," the guy had the nerve to mouth next to his ear.

Then he moved around to Megan's back.

Gus saw him hesitate then smile very slightly as he tied her wrists together.

And there they were: cheek to cheek, neck to neck, chest to glorious chest and...crotch to crotch.

Barry began to sweat with the effort of ignoring all the places he was touching her. It was torture, that's what it was. And Gus knew it.

"And now, buddy, I've gotta take your cell phone." Gus unclipped it from Barry's belt.

Megan twisted so she could see Gus, giving Barry a preview of just how bad this was going to be.

"Now this one, I'm just going to take out the battery." He slipped the wafer off of Barry's phone and crushed it with his heel. He held up Megan's old-style phone. "Blondie, you're a cop. You should be ashamed of yourself."

"Don't break it! I only finished paying that off last year!"

Gus winced and shook his head as he walked over to the workbench, put Megan's phone in a vice grip and tightened it until the plastic splintered.

Megan wailed right in Barry's ear. "I had phone numbers programmed in there!"

"Sorry." Gus opened his wallet, removed three bills and tucked them in the pocket of Megan's hoodie. "Buy yourself a new phone. Get one with a camera in it. I don't like the idea of cops wandering around with outdated equipment."

He stood and looked down at them, grinned wolfishly at Barry and left. "Your purse is by the door, blondie," he called before disappearing into the dusk.

6

Barry stared after him.

"How much money did he give me?" Megan asked.

"We're tied up in a deserted airplane hangar and you're only interested in the money?"

"Not *only*."

Barry twisted until he could see a corner peeking from Megan's pocket. "Looks like he gave you three hundred bucks."

Megan beamed. "That was nice of him."

"Nice? *Nice?* He tied us up!"

"Yeah, but he didn't shoot us."

Which proved to be a conversation killer as they both contemplated what could have been. And without the talking, Barry was feeling. Oh, boy, was he feeling. Megan, with her torso pressed against him and her hair tickling his nose and her legs wrapped around him, was triggering strong feelings. More like urges. Urges of which she was unaware, and which she clearly didn't reciprocate.

Gus had done this on purpose. He'd known *exactly* what effect tying them in this position would have.

Megan's head was bowed so Barry couldn't see her eyes and she kept wiggling. If they weren't tied up, he'd call it shimmying. He was going to call it that anyway. *Shimmying.*

"Are you uncomfortable?" he asked.

"Duh."

"I meant other than being tied up."

She looked up at him and laughed. "You mean am I uncomfortable with the fact that we're plastered up against each other?"

That was direct. "Well, yeah."

She stopped moving, allowing his brain to clear a bit. Then she gave him that tiny smile—the one he'd seen earlier. The one that made his blood run cold. And hot. And fast.

"Oh, I don't know," she said, her mouth just a breath away from his. "I'm enjoying being this close to you." She held his gaze for a second more before undulating her shoulders again.

Barry felt dizzy, but that could have been because he'd stopped breathing. That was such an un-Megan-like thing to say. He tried to swallow and found he wasn't any more successful at that, either.

"I—" He had to clear his throat. "I haven't seen this, er, earthier side of you before."

She looked up, her hair falling into her eyes in a sexy bed-tousled way. "Just because you haven't seen it doesn't mean it's not there."

Barry felt crucial wiring in his brain short-circuit. Random partial thoughts formed and fizzled. "I-i-if you could just stop moving for a little while…" The last came out in a ragged whisper.

"I *have* to move. How do you expect me…" She trailed off as she gazed into his eyes.

Who knows what she saw there—besides the lust.

Nothing. Because there was nothing *but* lust.

Barry stared down at her knowing the balance of power between them was sliding her way. His only hope now was that she wouldn't realize it.

She blinked and something shifted in her expression.

She realized it. *Please be gentle.*

"Oh, come on. Go ahead and enjoy." She pointedly looked down between them before tossing her hair back. "Relax. Men are just hardwired to respond in a situation like this."

She had that half-right.

"I'm not going to hold basic biology against you."

"The holding against me part is what I like." He smiled. He didn't know what kind of smile because he hadn't planned it. A rarity for him.

She grinned back. "That's the Barry I know."

"But you're not the Megan I know."

She shook her head. "You don't know me at all. You never looked behind the uniform."

That's what *she* thought.

"I'm more than my job—or what my job was."

Yeah, well that worked both ways. "We all are."

Megan peered up at him. "I don't think you are. Not that much, anyway."

Barry tried to be insulted but decided she was right.

"Or if you are, the real you is too deeply hidden." She tossed her head, trying to get a piece of hair out of her face. "The only time I ever see something I think might be the real you is when someone acts differently than you've predicted they would act. But even then, you have a fast recovery."

"What do you see when it's the real me?" he couldn't help asking.

"Somebody who cares. Someone who's vulnerable."

In other words, a wimp. "Oh, that sounds sexy."

"It's okay to care, Barry. And, yes, it can be sexy."

"Who says I don't care? I care about stuff. I just care about some stuff more than other stuff."

"Not stuff. People. You don't want anyone to know you might actually care, so you put up a big front."

"Everybody puts up a front."

"Not constantly. At some point, they have to be themselves or they'll never have meaningful relationships."

Sooner or later, women always talked about "relationships." "I think a little mystery is good for a relationship."

"But the mystery shouldn't be the true identity of a person in the relationship."

She saw too much. "I'm not a fake, if that's what you're implying. I changed myself."

"Why?"

Barry answered her with a burst of raw honesty. "So people would like me." He'd never admitted that to anyone.

She blinked at him from beneath a wave of hair. "Are you saying people don't like you once they get to know you? Maybe there's a reason."

"It's more that they don't bother to get to know me. The me I was, anyway. It's a long story."

A deep rumble began. The plane's engines were warming up.

Megan sighed. "I may have time to hear it. I doubt anyone is going to come back here for a while."

"At least Gus didn't gag us." Barry was more than glad to change the subject. He'd completely lost control of the conversation.

"And what does that tell you?" Megan shouted over the deafening sound.

"He's sloppy?" Barry shouted back.

"It means no one will be around to hear us!" Megan mouthed.

As the roaring filled his ears, Barry just watched her mouth. She was still saying something, but he had no idea what. She had a great mouth. Why hadn't he noticed before? There was a lot he hadn't noticed about Megan before. He'd summed her up as a certain type, then had stopped seeing her, the way he did everybody. He wished he hadn't, but who knew she'd be worth really getting to know?

The plane roared off and Megan tossed her head again, flicking him in the face with her hair. "Darn it!"

"Here. Let me." Waiting until she stilled, Barry slowly leaned forward and caught the strand of hair that was bothering her between his lips. He recognized the bitter taste of hair spray or finishing spritz or whatever it was called now, but ignored it to savor the feel of Megan's cheek against his lips. He liked being this close to her. Wouldn't mind being closer. Emotionally closer.

The thought started his heart pounding and it took

all his willpower not to abandon his task and kiss her and hope to heck she kissed him back.

But she trusted him to behave in the situation in which they found themselves. She was being very adult about it. Very matter-of-fact. The sexual-attraction switch was flipped off.

Only Barry couldn't turn off his switch. He didn't even want to try. He wanted to touch her so badly he feared he'd do something supremely idiotic.

So he concentrated on moving his lips across her cheek and nudging the strand of hair behind her ear. A small piece started to fall and he caught it, his tongue flicking out and touching the tip of her ear. Desire tore through him.

Megan's breath hitched and for an instant, Barry considered abandoning his good intentions and diving wholeheartedly into his bad intentions.

If this had been a woman other than Megan, he would have, but Megan wouldn't like it and that mattered to him. With another woman, Barry would charm her into forgiving him afterward. He didn't want to resort to charm with Megan. Slowly, he inched his face away from her cheek. "Better?"

"Yes, thanks," she whispered.

They stared at each other. Neither of them moved. Barry wished Megan would say something, *do* something. Holding himself in check was the most he could manage just now.

"And thank you for not saying 'I told you so,'" she said.

"About what?"

"The groom is definitely up to something."

"Oh, yeah. That."

"*Oh yeah, that?* You've been pushing all day and now it's 'oh yeah, that'?"

"Got other stuff on my mind right now."

Like feeling light-headed because he'd been taking too many shallow breaths to avoid touching any more of Megan than was strictly necessary. He risked a deep breath. He had to.

Beauty-salon smell filled his nostrils and a uniquely feminine softness pillowed his chest. Right this minute, he didn't care if they ever escaped.

"What's on your mind?" She looked down at herself. "These?"

Barry exhaled in a rush. "Uh, yeah." He should say something more than that, but it had to be the right something and he couldn't read her the way he used to. He couldn't think the way he used to, either.

She was still looking down. "They are *always* getting in the way."

Barry tried not to whimper. "They're…" He searched for a word. "Magnificent. You have magnificent breasts," he managed to say. Not his best, but not too bad.

Megan stopped struggling with her wrists and blinked up at him. "Oh, please. You don't think that way."

"Actually—"

"With men, it's either 'great tits' or 'nice rack' or 'what a set of gazongas' or 'hooters' or 'jugs' or 'knockers'—"

"Boobs," he interrupted. "That would be my noun of choice. But it didn't go with 'magnificent.'"

"Oh." She breathed for a minute, her magnificence ebbing and flowing against him. "I guess that's not so bad. I've heard worse."

"I can tell."

She sighed down at herself. "They're a lot of trouble, especially in softball. And I have to pay extra for my uniform shirts to be tailored."

"You've always looked professional." Stacked, but professional.

She smiled up at him. "And you always made eye contact when we talked, Barry. I noticed and I appreciated that."

Don't say it. Don't say it. "I have really great peripheral vision." He said it.

A corner of her mouth kicked upward. "So do I. You've got a nice ass."

His blood started doing the hot-and-cold thing again. Being tied to her would be so much easier if she hated him. As it was, he was assessing the romantic possibilities of the oil-stained concrete floor of an airplane hangar. Not good.

"Okay, enough of this. You'd better lean back or I might knock you in the chin with my head," Megan said with the matter-of-factness he'd admired earlier—before he'd known her peripheral vision had been checking him out.

"I'll do my best." Barry leaned back a couple of inches, all he could do since her feet were tied together behind him. "So now what?"

"I'm trying to get loose. You know, at first, when Gus grabbed me? He countered my defense moves before I had a chance to make them. I knew right then that he was a seasoned pro. But when I crossed my hands behind me, I did it in a way that would leave me some room to slip my wrists apart. And he didn't catch it. How to secure a suspect is one of the first things we learned and it was drilled into us. I can't believe somebody with his experience would let me keep my hands in that position."

Barry thought back to Gus's smile when he secured Megan's hands. "I think he caught it and just let it go."

"You do? Why?"

"Why did he give you money for a new cell phone? I sure didn't see that coming."

She looked off to the side as she considered it. "I could say he was trying to bribe an officer."

"But you won't."

She shook her head. "Nope. I figure he's involved in something way bigger than the Dallas PD will get to handle."

"Ya think?" That was what Barry had been trying to convince people of all day.

"Yeah. That Learjet that just took off? That wasn't the Hargrove Security Systems plane. That's gotta be a loaner. My guess is that he intends to put some serious miles on it tonight."

"How do you know it isn't Hargrove's plane?" Barry asked.

"That's not the one in the database. And of course, there was the discreet silver-and-black Sterling International logo on the side."

How had he missed that? "Makes sense. The groomsmen said they overheard Gus talking with his best man about planes." Barry's reporter's instincts—diverted briefly by more basic instincts—woke up. "This story has got to be huge. Gus started Hargrove over a year ago, so he presumably broke ties with Sterling before that. For Derek to pull him away from his wedding means something major is going down. Megan, if we break it, we'll be back in the game. And you know what else?"

"Um."

"I'm thinking good ole Congressman Galloway is up to his neck in it."

"In a good way or a bad way?"

"That's what I need to figure out." Figuring it out would be a good thing. It would be a distracting thing.

And right now, with Megan rubbing against him as she struggled to free herself, Barry needed a really good distraction.

MEGAN HAD LISTENED to Barry babble his theories incessantly. "You know more about that investigation we were busted for than you told me, don't you?" he asked not for the first time.

Please shut up. Just shut up. It was bad enough to be in such forced intimacy—quite frankly one of her fantasies before she'd learned that it was painful—without listening to Barry's blathering.

She'd flirted with him. That was progress for her. He'd really been off balance. She'd never *ever* used her sexuality that way before. And then she'd spoiled it by whining about her boobs. It's just that she didn't know how to make the most of having them.

She bet Barry would.

No, no, *no*. She couldn't think that way. Mustn't think that way. Sure, Barry found her attractive *now*, but once they were untied, that would be the end of it for him.

But she'd have memories this time. She'd know how it felt to be pressed against his chest and how his mouth felt against her cheek. She wanted to bury her nose in the crook of his neck and just breathe.

And she wanted one really great kiss out of the deal. Just one. A long one. Was that asking too much?

As she half listened to Barry pose theories and then try to answer them without any input from her, Megan was grateful that he had either ignored or let slide how they'd come to be in this situation. Personally, she was horrified. Good grief. She'd been caught like a rookie. No, she didn't have the street experience of some of her colleagues, but she sure was no rookie. And she'd grown up with a couple of wily brothers. No excuse. None.

The only way to get over her embarrassment and redeem herself was to get them out of this mess.

She should have thought it through before she'd started moving her wrists because now they were swollen, which didn't make things easier. She was trying to flatten one hand and sort of fold the other to shift the plastic strip down the back of her hand. If she could just find the right angle, she'd have it, but she was so close to Barry she couldn't lean forward the way she wanted to.

If he'd just *shut up*, she could concentrate.

She felt a slickness run down her wrists and the plastic bonds slide a little. Finally.

"So I'm thinking we ought to try to find Derek. If he's not at the rehearsal dinner—which has got to have started by now—then he's with Gus. And there was a bachelor party scheduled for after the dinner. Can't have a bachelor party without the bachelor—"

"How good are your abs?" she interrupted Barry. Judging from this position, she figured they were flat and hard, but he could just be skinny.

"I do my share of crunches," he said casually.

Just like her brothers. This meant he probably did a couple hundred every morning, after which he spent an equal amount of time examining himself in the mirror. "Great. I want you to lean back and hold the position so I can get some leverage, but don't go back too far or my ankles will hurt."

He looked stricken. "Are you in pain?"

Wasn't he? "I'm fine. I'm just mad."

"I thought Gus was your new best friend since he updated your cell phone."

Megan shifted because her butt was going numb on the cold concrete. "He sneaked up on me and I don't like knowing I can be sneaked up on."

"You know, it might be time to let that go. It happened. Move on."

"Okay." She took a deep breath and watched Mr. Fabulous-Peripheral-Vision's eyes flick down to her chest.

For once, she didn't mind. "Lean back."

He did so. "Enough?"

Oh, yes. Nice abs. Megan bent forward at her waist, her nose even with the midpoint of his chest.

She risked a glance upward. There was his mouth. She sighed. "Yeah, I think this will do it."

She pulled. Her shoulders were sore since pulling free involved putting her wrists more perpendicular than was comfortable and strained the muscles. Her hand began to work free. Almost there…

Her delts started cramping. "Ow!" She relaxed immediately to head off the cramp, felt her hand slip back and lost all her hard-won progress.

Groaning, she collapsed against Barry's chest. She couldn't help it—she was exhausted and hurting, not that she needed a reason.

"Megan?"

"I'm okay," she mumbled against his shirt.

As he moved back into a sitting position, she just slid up until her head rested on his shoulder.

She was gearing up for another round of struggling when Barry unexpectedly pressed his lips against her forehead.

"You're fantastic, you know that?" he murmured.

She was? Startled, Megan looked up.

"Other women would not be handling this at all well. And you just…just…"

His mouth was nearly touching hers. She didn't move. Maybe this was it.

His eyes looked into hers with intent. Yeah, this was definitely it.

And then he kissed her. Truly. A for-real kiss.

Sure, her lips were in the vicinity and he was only taking advantage of the situation, she knew that. Why shouldn't she do likewise? She'd wanted one really great kiss and now seemed like a good time. Actually, since he was already kissing her, now would be a *great* time.

Megan leaned into him and fit her mouth firmly against his. Barry responded by expertly taking their kiss to the next level.

Oh. Wow.

Barry's next level was a level she didn't experience very often.

His lips settled against hers in a way that said, *We're going to be here awhile so let's explore*. And she parted her lips so he could take the grand tour of her mouth.

This was one of those kisses that told a girl the guy would be a faboo lover. An all-around great first kiss. No banging of the teeth because one of the parties was more enthusiastic than the other. Nothing too sloppily passionate that would make eye contact afterward awkward. Not that passion didn't have its place, but its place was not an airplane hangar while they were tied together.

Barry tilted his head and she kind of clicked into place. Her nerves hummed. Actually, they were singing complete arias mostly consisting of words like *yes* and *more* and *don't stop*.

Okay. Okay, maybe Megan could be talked out of her position that this wasn't the place for passion. She was feeling that passion was very appropriate right now. She forgot all about her cold backside and her sore shoulders and her bound wrists. There was only Barry and his slow, exploratory kiss. He was finding out what she liked—pretty much everything—and sending wave after wave of shivers down her spine.

After this, Barry would be entitled to brag that he

could out-kiss any man with both hands tied behind his back—literally. Megan was grateful hands weren't involved. Dealing with the kiss all by itself was plenty.

Then Barry threw in some great tongue moves and Megan went all boneless against him, which had an added side effect—the plastic binding slipped down to the knuckles of one hand. She wiggled her fingers and was free.

Kissing as an escape tactic—who knew?

In her newly wanton state—it must be the hair—Megan didn't immediately inform Barry that she was free.

What was another minute—or three? She'd wanted a good, long kiss to remember him by. And maybe, just maybe, he'd remember her, too.

But all good things must end, darn it. And she'd end the kiss, too, just as soon as she thought of something sophisticated and witty and just the slightest bit racy to say. Or at least anything non-dorky.

She pulled back, ready with her witty remark, but the dazed heat on Barry's face stopped her.

She was expecting Barry to have a sort of yeah-I'm-good-but-you-weren't-so-bad-yourself expression, a look both confident and sweet. After all, she was beginning to realize that Barry had an underlying sweetness beneath his manipulations. And, man, was he ever entitled to the I'm-good part of the look.

The I've-been-hit-in-the-head-by-a-baseball-bat thing he had going couldn't have been planned. "Megan," he whispered.

Damn it. Right kiss, wrong time.

"Hold that thought," she whispered back. Wiggling her shoulders, she gave him a brilliant, toothy smile. "Look!" She held up her hands.

Horror crossed his features. "That's blood!"

She looked at her wrists. Not attractive. "Well, yeah. I was using it as a lubricant."

"Megan." He jerked his shoulders and she knew he'd involuntarily reached for her, forgetting that his hands were tied. Yup, sweet. "That's awful." His face hardened. "The guy is a jerk."

"It's okay. It worked." Except now there wasn't anything to wipe her hands on since she'd used the tissue in her pocket after looking under the hood of Barry's car. She did have more tissues in her purse, but that wasn't doing her any good right now. Finally, she blotted her fingertips on the side of her jeans and ruined her manicure by picking the zipper pull tab off her hoodie.

Barry had been very quiet—yeah, *now* he was quiet. It appeared discussing the kiss was off-limits. And what could they say? *Hey, we kissed. Hey, it was good. Hey, let's do it again?*

No. This was a one-time memory maker. A diversion.

"What are you doing?" he asked.

"I need something sharp to get you loose. The tie wraps have a tab that locks them in place. If you pry it up, they'll slip open."

Once she'd removed the metal zipper pull, Megan looked up at him. "I'm going to reach around you."

She leaned forward and wrapped her arms around his waist, laying her cheek against his chest.

She felt his heart beating and gave herself an extra second to just enjoy before searching for the tie wrap at his wrists and freeing him.

"Thanks." Exhaling in relief, Barry moved his arms and Megan had to sit up.

"Your hands are purple!" Before, she'd been annoyed at Gus. Now, after seeing Barry's hands and the angry red welts at his wrists, she was furious.

"They went numb a little while ago." He rubbed at them. "They'll be okay." He gazed at her and Megan restrained herself from touching his jaw.

This was the point where they would either forget everything and kiss again or—

"I guess I should disentangle myself," he said.

So he was going with "or"—literally as well as figuratively disentangling. Though it was what she'd expected, *wanted* even, she was still disappointed. "That would be the next step."

Even though it was for the best, Megan was almost sorry when he maneuvered himself away from her and she could free her ankles.

Barry retrieved her purse and dug in it for the tissues. "I am going to get that guy," he threatened darkly. "Big secret government spy or not, he *will* pay."

Barry in revenge mode was sexy, if unrealistic. Megan dabbed at the drying blood on her wrists. "Barry, this is real life, not a story."

He laughed without humor. "Real life is a story. I'm going to find out what Gus's is." Then, surprising them both, he took her hands and placed a kiss on each of Megan's wrists.

She could feel herself melting. Not good. "Barry..."

He gazed at her, his famous smile absent. "I'm so sorry I got you into this."

He genuinely was. Megan could tell. And somehow, Barry being genuinely contrite was worse than Barry being fake contrite. Deliberately breaking the mood, she tugged her hands away. "I didn't have anything else to do."

"Still." Barry let her hands go and eyed her. "I want to find out where Gus is headed."

"And I want to go home," Megan said. She'd had too much Barry recently. Barry's stock in trade was being extremely likable and Megan knew she had to be careful not to like him too much.

"Go home? How can you want to go home when things are just getting exciting?"

Megan headed for the hangar door. "What happened to 'I'm sorry I got you into this mess'?"

"Yeah, but since you're already in it, you might as well see it through."

"I've had enough excitement for one day." Megan jerked at the huge sliding metal door. "Come on."

Though he helped her pull open the door, Barry still tried to convince her. "Could we at least talk to the FBO people before we leave?"

She gave him a look.

"And, okay, if you'd flash your badge around, it would help."

He was incorrigible. Megan continued to stare at him.

"The cards." Barry gestured toward her purse. "Hand them over."

What a good idea. She'd forgotten about the Barry

aversion therapy. Megan blindly withdrew a card. "You promised me dinner after I worked late getting you clearance to print a feature article." Oh, this was good. She remembered now. She remembered ordering two very expensive drinks and being sized up by every man who bellied up to the bar. "I was to meet you at the Florida Grill for seafood. I sat in the bar for an hour and a half." And was only hit on once, not that she wanted to be hit on, but still.

Barry's face was blank.

"You don't even remember."

"Not until just now." He took the card from her. "I'm sorry." That was all he said. He looked at her, letting the apology sink in. Then he crooked a smile at her. "Hungry now?"

"Yes, as a matter of fact."

"Okay, I'll feed you before taking you home. Probably not the Florida Grill, though."

She'd take it and she wouldn't point out that she was the one driving the car. "Deal."

"Okay, then." He ripped up the card. "Another one. One card for each wrist."

Megan took another card. Actually, Barry had promised her coffee that, on more than one occasion, hadn't materialized. She hoped she hadn't picked one of those cards. "Ah. You embarrassed me at a press briefing."

"So?"

"*So?* When the mayor was looking for a new police chief, you asked me questions in a way that made me look stupid in front of everybody. They didn't believe what I was saying!"

"That's my job! I'm supposed to figure out whether the pap you're spouting is true or propaganda. Give me the card."

He snatched it from her unresisting fingers and tore it up without apologizing. "Any others like that?"

Megan silently shuffled through the index cards and weeded out all the ones when a question from Barry had flustered her because it had pointed out illogicality in the official statements she'd been given. Illogicality that she should have caught instead of blindly believing everything she'd been told.

Barry ripped them up, then looked at the smaller stack that was left. "See? I'm not such a bad guy."

Speaking of logic, what kind of logic was that? Yet, somehow, Megan found herself agreeing to go with him to the FBO office and lend her "official" help. Help she hoped wasn't questioned.

Under the glow of pink halogen lights, they walked to the building. Through the smoked windows lining the front, Megan saw an actual chandelier, art on the walls, carpeting and enough potted palms to start a nursery. It looked like a hotel lobby instead of a place to fuel private airplanes.

"Let me do the talking," Barry said when they spotted a security guard. "You get your badge ready."

The way he dealt with the security guard was frightening, really. Barry never actually claimed to be a police detective, yet the way he referred to Megan, who dutifully produced her credentials when required, might have led one to assume that they were both police officers. *Might* being the operative word, the word making their actions defensible if they should need defending, which Megan hoped they wouldn't.

He was really good, but she knew that. She was getting an excellent lesson in presentation and decided just to go with it rather than assert her right to do the talking. Megan did remember to keep the sleeves of her hoodie pulled down to cover her wrists. She didn't want anyone questioning them.

And so, within minutes, they were looking at the flight-plan logbook. Again, ominously easy.

"Washington D.C." Barry glanced at her before thanking the manager and putting his hand in the small of her back to steer Megan out the door.

"Police officers do not touch each other like that," Megan whispered after they stepped outside. "You made me appear to be weaker and subordinate."

He flashed a grin at her. "Good thing I'm not a police officer."

"Barry."

"Okay. Noted. But hey, I was on the money about Washington D.C. So, what do you think? Galloway's got to be involved." He was walking so fast, they might as well have been jogging to her car.

"Just because Gus and whoever are headed to Washington D.C. doesn't mean the congressman is involved," Megan said, trying to convince him.

"Yes, it does." Barry was clearly unconvinceable. "We'll grab a couple of burgers and bounce theories off each other."

Oh, joy. The dinner she was owed.

Barry reached into his jacket pocket and hissed through his teeth. "No cell phone. Nuts."

But Megan was staring ahead of them. "We've got worse problems. Check out my car."

"That looks familiar," Barry said.

There sat the car, right where they'd parked it, all four tires flat.

7

MEGAN SNEAKED ONE of Barry's fries. She'd already eaten all of hers. "I can't believe my car tires are filled with nitrogen."

Barry didn't look up from his laptop. "You should be glad. Didn't you hear what the mechanic said? The molecules are larger, so they won't go through the rubber as fast. Your tires will stay inflated longer."

"Yeah, yeah, yeah." Megan squirted ketchup onto the greasy paper of her empty red plastic basket. Actually, the airplane-tire service-cart mechanic had been very nice, assuring Megan that he "topped off" car tires all the time. Even so, once she saw the pressure gauges on the nitrogen canisters, Megan had visions of exploding tires right up until the last one on her car had been safely inflated.

Barry nudged his basket of fries across the table of their booth. "And I notice Gus didn't take any engine parts off *your* car."

Megan dunked a bundle of stolen fries into the ketchup all at once. "He likes me better."

Barry glanced up at that and Megan remembered him blathering on about not being liked when he was younger.

She swallowed her handful and then salted his fries. "I'm kidding. He figured you, as a manly man, knew all about mechanics, whereas I, a helpless female, wouldn't know what to do."

Barry went back to his laptop. "It doesn't matter if you know what to do with it if you don't have it to do it with."

Megan munched on a fry. "You've got a good editor, don't you?"

"You know what I meant."

And she did. They were sitting in a mottled green plastic booth, breathing the grease-laden air of Bonnie's Burger Basket. When Barry had directed her to pull in here, she'd assumed it was one of his haunts, maybe a cool place where reporters hung out when they were on a late-night deadline.

But he'd never been here. No, he'd smelled the place while driving by a couple of days ago. And this counted as the big dinner he owed her. Still, Megan wasn't exactly disappointed. She didn't know what she felt. Or maybe it was that she didn't feel the way she thought she should feel. While Barry surfed the Web and Megan ate the rest of his fries, she thought about how Gina would react when Megan told her about dinner with Barry. Her co-worker would assume Megan would be insulted by Barry's casualness in choosing a place to eat. The truth was, well, Megan didn't feel insulted.

True, the eatery was in a less desirable part of Dallas near Love Field. The smell of frying from Bonnie's permeated the neighborhood, acting as its best advertisement. Houses surrounded the commercial oasis, which consisted of a laundromat, a video-rental place, a combination convenience store and gas station and finally Bonnie's Burger Basket. And actually, if you were going to eat grease, this was one of the best places to do it.

It was just that she hadn't planned to eat quite so much of it. Judging from Barry's quick glance at his rapidly disappearing fries, he hadn't expected her to, either.

"Oh, give me a break," Megan grumbled. "There was a piece of lettuce and a tomato slice in my hamburger. Salad."

"I didn't say anything."

"And that's the problem. Why didn't you say, 'Hey, Megan, don't eat all my fries'?"

"'Cause if I want more fries, I'll order more fries. Anyway, you let me have your pickles."

She wished he wouldn't be reasonable like that. "I got the better deal."

He gave her a quick, preoccupied smile. She waited for him to say something. When he didn't, Megan ate another fry and thought that this was the third different kind of smile in a row from him. He wasn't trying to manipulate her the way he used to. Or was he just using more devious means?

"Barry?"

He stared, trancelike, at the computer monitor. "Mmm?"

"When you told me people didn't like you as a kid, was that true?"

He exhaled and pushed back from the computer. "It was more that I didn't ping their radar. People pretty much ignored me."

Megan studied his face. Right. "You cannot convince me that you weren't one of the cool kids."

Barry blinked at her, then shifted in the seat until he could remove his wallet. Opening it, he gazed down for a second before removing a photograph and sliding it across the table to her. "My family."

Megan's attention was immediately captured by the three young women in long gowns. Whoa. Where was the picture taken—the Miss Texas pageant? They all had long dark hair, white smiles and perfect posture. They were the kind of effortlessly beautiful girls who made Megan feel her most inadequate. Their aura would blind men to any other female in the vicinity.

"Your sisters?"

"Yes."

And these were the type of women who'd imprinted themselves on Barry's psyche as the female prototype. They were anti-Megans. Beautiful and high maintenance. No wonder he knew his way around a salon better than she did.

Megan forced her attention away from the stunning gorgeousness of Barry's sisters to study the other people in the photo. She saw an attractive older couple, who would be his parents, and, like a dark blot among the radiant pastel gowns, a geeky teenager in a black suit and unfortunate white socks. He had a huge nose, no chin, a Brillo pad for hair, and a mouthful of metal, which he displayed in a huge grin. "Is this your little broth—oh, my gosh, that's you!" She looked up at him and back to the picture. "It is you, isn't it?"

His face was blank. "Yeah."

"What did you do to yourself?"

"Nothing."

"Oh, come on." Megan held up the photo and compared Barry's face to the picture. The picture was only wallet-size, but you couldn't miss a big nose and no chin. "You got your nose fixed, didn't you?"

He shook his head.

"Let me see your profile."

Barry dutifully turned to the side.

"Okay, no, you didn't. No self-respecting plastic surgeon would have left that bump in the middle."

"Gee thanks."

Frankly, the nose, well, was a honker, but honestly it fit Barry's face. "Your nose is great." Megan waved her hand. "Don't ever have it fixed. If you did, you'd be too pretty. Now, you're handsome and handsome is always more interesting than pretty." She squinted at the picture. "I know—you had a chin implant. There's no way you could have grown a jaw like that from what you looked like in this picture."

"But I did."

"Oh, *sure* you did. Tilt your head back. I'm checking for scars."

"Megan!" A laugh escaped as he tilted back his head.

A telltale white jagged line marred the shadow of his beard. He pointed to it. "This is from knocking my chin on the side of a swimming pool."

"Oh, *okay.*" Megan gave him an exaggerated wink. "I get it."

"It is. Besides, chin implants are often done internally so there aren't visible scars—not that I have any internal scars either," he quickly added.

The chin scar did look pretty sloppy for a surgical scar. "Wow." Megan lowered the picture and stared at him. "So you like, got your braces off and, boom, you were gorgeous?"

The bemused way Barry looked at her made Megan think there was something she was missing that he hoped she wouldn't discover.

"It took a few years for my face to catch up to my nose. I was a late bloomer."

When he bloomed, he bloomed. She handed him back his picture. "Oh, it more than caught up. I mean, I know you're more than your looks, but Barry, when you walk by, women have to grab onto something because their knees have gone weak. I know for a fact that in the station, there have been actual incidences of drooling. You know, it was always fun to see the reactions of the new women reporters when they first saw you. They'd just stare and forget to ask questions. Which you use to your advantage. I know you do. Even I, who know what you look like, find it hard to concentrate sometimes. You'll ask me something and I'll just zone out because you're smiling one of your dimple smiles. It's on one of the cards."

Megan licked her finger after pressing it into the bottom of the basket to capture stray salt and bits of fries. "You know the time you wore a tuxedo to the Policeman's Ball? You had your hair slicked back, which normally doesn't do it for me, but a couple of little curls right here—" she touched her temples "—were rebelling and you looked *so cute*. And hot. At the same time. Bad boy in a tux." She sighed at the memory. "A great look. I was, for the only time in my

life, envied by other women because you spoke to
me. Unfortunately, you were only asking for
information, but they didn't know that. And I babbled and babbled because, oh, gosh, I wanted you to
ask me to dance *so bad,* I thought I would just…"
Megan became aware of Barry's slightly raised eyebrows and the fact that he'd said absolutely nothing
for a very long time. "Die." Like right now. "I said all
that out loud, didn't I?" she whispered.

"Uh-huh," he whispered back.

Maybe if she stayed very still the last few minutes
would evaporate or she'd wake up, or… Or nothing.
It's not like her finding him attractive was a total surprise after the kiss. The kiss they weren't discussing.

Barry closed his notebook computer. "Card." He
gestured with his fingers.

Megan knew the card he wanted. Conscious of
his gaze on her, she shuffled through the diminish-
ing pile until she found the tux card. Without read-
ing it, he tore it up.

Fishing in his pocket for change, he turned his attention to the tabletop jukebox. "You an Elvis fan?"

"I…Elvis is Elvis."

"And that's plenty." Barry shoved quarters into
the coin slot and punched a selection.

Bonnie's Burger Basket filled with the heavy, liq-
uid-velvet sound of Elvis singing, "I Can't Help Falling in Love With You." Barry stood and held out his
hand to her.

He wasn't in a tux and she wasn't wearing the
black dress she'd borrowed from Gina, but Megan
took his hand anyway.

Barry pulled her into his arms and swayed slowly in time to the music. If Megan closed her eyes, and she did, then she could imagine that it was the night of the Policeman's Ball. Only this was better.

Better than being tied together, too.

Maybe not better than the kiss, but pretty darn close.

They weren't the only people in Bonnie's Burger Basket, but Megan didn't care. Barry was dancing with her. And he could dance, too, which didn't surprise Megan. She just settled her cheek against his shoulder and followed his lead. He was being sweet and hokey and achingly romantic and darn it, the song was appropriate.

Because she couldn't help falling in love with him.

HE'D INTENDED TO ASK HER to dance that night, but he'd had to file his story. By the time Barry had returned to the ballroom, she'd left.

Megan felt good in his arms. And she liked him. She didn't want to, but she did. And the part she didn't want to like was the part everyone else did like.

She'd talked about the "real" Barry, but no one ever paid any attention to the "real" Barry. Even now, he could fade into the background anytime he wished and wait for the unguarded comments that enriched his stories.

He'd grown up in the shadow of his pretty and popular sisters. Tired of being overlooked, he'd tried different personalities until he found the one people most responded to and that was the one they got.

He'd studied books on body language, subliminal communication, sales techniques and persuasive speaking. He'd absorbed and practiced everything until it had become automatic. Until it had become a part of him.

And Megan had seen through it all.

Barry had always hoped to meet a woman who would see through his careful facade, but since he never chanced revealing himself, he'd figured it was unlikely.

Sure, he'd known that someday he'd have to drop his usual tactics and peel away the layers of carefully cultivated charm until the woman either ran screaming into the night, or stuck around. And only when the risk of rejection was past, would Barry allow himself to fall in love.

But here was Megan, just putting herself out there, revealing her feelings, revealing herself, fully aware of how he worked people and yet, she was still here. Still in his arms.

He'd chosen the song on purpose because even though it wasn't safe until Megan really knew him, Barry couldn't help falling in love with her.

Wise? No. Exciting? Definitely. He relived a few moments of their soul-jarring kiss in the airplane hangar. Basically, he'd been looking to scratch a sexual itch, but at the first touch of her mouth, the emotions had just poured through him, filling all the dry cracks in his heart. So, yeah. How could he help falling for her?

It was amazing. As the minutes had gone by and he'd held her in his arms, he'd just fallen in love. She'd never believe him—*he* didn't believe him. But he definitely had to kiss her again and soon.

The song ended long before Barry was ready for it to. He held Megan until the last note faded away. Slowly, they parted and Megan gave him a shy smile. Shy? After the way she'd kissed him earlier?

Maybe that's why, Sherlock.

"Thanks, Barry."

He should be thanking her. He cleared his throat. "So. You still want to go home, or do you want to hang out with me some more?" If he wanted to, Barry could convince her, but he wanted it to be her choice.

"If I don't hang out with you, you won't have a chauffeur."

"Borrowing another car is not a problem." *Say it.* He hesitated. This revealing stuff was hard. "I want to spend more time with you."

"Really?" Her face lit with what he would call guarded enthusiasm. Not a rousing endorsement.

"Really." And it would be best if she didn't know how much.

She studied him and letting her do so without verbally twisting her arm was an effort.

"I need to know why you want to spend time with me."

And *this* was why relationships had always been too much trouble for him. He should have read a how-to book on those as well. Okay. He could do this. "I like you. You have a different outlook than my sisters—than a lot of women. I want to get to know you better. And I want you to know me better."

She grinned. "You're going to let me get to know your inner geek?"

He rubbed the space between his eyebrows. What

happened to her not talking so much? "Uh, I suppose you could put it that way."

She headed back to the table. "Don't panic. I like geeks."

"Hey!" Barry followed. "I'm not the guy in the picture anymore, if that's what you're thinking."

She picked up her purse. "So who kissed me?"

"What do you mean?" He zipped the case on his laptop.

"In the airplane hangar. Was it oh-so-charming Barry, going through his moves, or was it the shy but sincere geek?"

So she'd figured out that he calculated kisses, as well. "Oh, that was Mr. Smooth Moves, himself," he admitted. "The geek never kissed anybody."

"Hmm." She looked off into the middle distance. "Well, if there's going to be more kissing, then bring Barry back."

He just never knew what she was going to say. But there was definitely going to be more kissing. Except that she was walking out of Bonnie's and he was looking at the back of her head instead of her mouth. So, later.

They got to her car and Barry wanted to drive, but Megan didn't seem the type of woman who'd relinquish the wheel. She wasn't a wimpy driver, so he could stand being driven.

"Where are we going now?" she asked. "Please don't say back to the hotel for the rehearsal dinner."

Since that's exactly where he wanted to go, Barry just gave her a look over the top of the car.

"Nooooo! I'm not dressed for it."

"You won't have to mingle with the guests. I only want to see if Derek is there or if he went on the plane with Gus."

"And then what?"

"And then I see what I can find out. Also, I want to know what they told Sally."

Megan groaned.

"Card?"

Megan dug around in her purse, then slid a card across the roof of the car before unlocking the door.

Barry got in the car and read the card. "Barry asked me for more information. I spent three hours getting it cleared and then he didn't use it in the article. Megan, there's no guarantee that anything gets into an article. For one thing, I have space limitations."

"It was a Friday night. I gave up a movie to do that for you and I'll bet you'd already written your story. You weren't there when I called. I left a message and I called again. And then the next morning, I had to go into the station to explain to the captain why *his* dinner had been interrupted for nothing."

Barry slowly tore the card. "So you're saying I owe you a movie?"

"*No!*" Megan banged her hands on the wheel. "I'm saying that you're thoughtless. Sometimes you just ask for stuff because you know you can. You never stop to think. What you do has an effect on people, but you're never around to see it. You just flash one of your smiles and skate on by and that's supposed to make everything okay."

Barry tried to see her point, but after all, she had been the department spokeswoman. Getting information to the press was her job. "Since I was unaware of your departmental procedures, I didn't realize that it had been such a hassle. Why didn't you say something?"

"And when was I supposed to?"

"Megan, I covered major crimes and you were the liaison—at least the one they trotted out when there were TV cameras."

"I object to the 'trotted out' crack."

"Sorry. But there were opportunities to say, 'Hey, getting information cleared is a hassle, so don't ask unless it's important.'"

Megan started the car. "And, naturally, you think everything is important."

"It usually is. Or was." Before he was put on wedding detail. "Next time, and I'm really hoping there's a next time, let me know if it's a problem because you know I'll be asking for everything I can get."

She gave him a direct look. "I know."

Did she expect him to apologize for doing his job? He wasn't going to. "Are we okay with that?"

When she nodded, he fastened his seat belt. "Speaking of getting information," he continued, "as long as we're at the rehearsal dinner, I should actually do my job. Talk to a few people."

"And what about me?"

"You can be my lookout."

"What am I looking out for?"

"You'll know it when you see it."

She rolled her eyes. "Oh, great."

"Megan?"

"What?"

How could he tell her that he liked the way she told him when she was mad about something? That she *cared* enough to tell him?

The thing was, nobody had ever really invested themselves in Barry. Not, he admitted, that he'd given anyone, particularly women, a chance. He knew he took shortcuts when he interacted with people but they never stuck around long enough for it to matter.

He thought about the index cards in Megan's purse and the fact that there had been so many of them. She was holding him accountable for his past actions. It mattered to her and he liked that.

He liked her. More than liked. But the problem with keeping things light, shallow and insincere all the time meant that when he was dark, deep and very, very sincere, he feared no one would believe him.

And then there was the kiss, the aftereffects of which were simmering just below the surface. Maybe closer to his surface than to her surface. He wanted to kiss her again as soon and for as long as possible.

Ultimately, all he said was, "Thanks."

Megan looked at him for a moment. Then, shaking her head, she backed out of the gravel parking lot. "Apparently I'm a sucker for your toned-down version, too."

Smiling to himself, he watched as she impatiently shoved a hank of hair behind one ear. She was so different from his sisters. Not that he disliked his sisters, but Megan appealed to him in a major way.

"How did you decide to become a police officer?" he asked.

She flipped her newly blond hair. "Where did that come from?"

"I'm trying to get to know the inner Megan."

"Oh, I'm me all the time. What you see is what you get. But I do understand why you slip into your super-Barry persona. I should get one of those."

"No. Don't."

She exhaled. "I need one because I feel awkward around most women. It's like there's a code I don't know. And it's not as though my mother wasn't a good example, but I just didn't get it. I was more interested in the stuff my brothers got to do and my parents let me do what I wanted. I always thought I'd just pick up the girlie stuff, but I never did." She made a dismissive gesture. "But back to your question. I sort of fell into law enforcement. I like working with the media and speaking to groups and this job came up with the police department. I figured that if I graduated from the academy, then I'd have an advantage over my competition because it would look better to the public to have a real officer representing the department. And I knew I could handle the physical requirements, so I applied to the academy and here I am. I never wanted to get into the law enforcement side. I believe that keeping the lines of communication open between the public and the police department is crucial and I also believe good communication enhances police effectiveness."

He loved it when she got all patriotic. "You sound like a press release."

"I know. I may have written that one. But I *do* believe it. I know what I do is important—what I did—

I'm not so sure where the blue pencils fit in all this—but I was good at what I did and darn it, I want my old job back."

Barry didn't know what the blue pencils were about, but he sincerely regretted that he'd contributed to her reprimand. At the time, he hadn't given any thought that she'd be blamed for the content of his story. Which had been the point she'd been making earlier.

"We're going to get your job back," he promised. "Mine, too."

She sighed heavily. "I don't know, Barry."

"No, see, we're going to figure out what's going on and how the congressman fits in and I'm going to write the story and you're getting a copy before it comes out in the newspaper. You will be the one who can respond because you're going to be right along with me. Got it? If the police want an effective public comment, it'll have to come from you. And if my paper wants the story, it'll have to be with my byline. Otherwise, I walk to the competition. How does that sound?"

She changed lanes back and forth to weave around a slower-moving pickup truck. "Too easy."

"I'm not saying it's going to be easy."

"At least promise me everything will be legal."

He thought about the congressman and he thought about Gus. Specifically a Gus who'd tied them up and destroyed his cell phone battery. He thought of the bloody cuts on Megan's wrists. "Define 'legal.'"

"Barry!"

"Do we need to go to the cards?"

"Barry, no card will make me do something illegal. I *am* a police officer and I *do* believe in upholding the law and I *will not* compromise my integrity."

That's my girl, he thought. "You can not possibly know how sexy you are when you start spouting 'truth, justice and the American way' propaganda."

"It's not propaganda!" Her voice rose. "And if you think so, then I'm pulling this car over right now and you can get out and walk!"

But she didn't slow down. "You know, I find it interesting that you ignored the 'sexy' part," he said. "You should never ignore the sexy part."

"Typical Barry."

"Nope. Not at all. I knew that would tick you off and I avoid irritating people."

"Then *why* say it?"

"You *do* look sexy when you're all passionate about what you believe in. Passion is always sexy. And after covering crime for so long, I'm cynical. I poked at you a little because I wanted to see your reaction. And I envy you your unshakable belief in the system."

EXCEPT THAT HER BELIEFS had been shaken. Not on the major stuff, but dealing with Barry's requests for information and irritating questions over the past couple of years had revealed some dubious aspects of law enforcement.

"I don't like people getting away with stuff," Megan said.

"And she still ignores the fact that twice I've called her sexy."

Oh, she hadn't ignored it. "Well what am I supposed to do about it? I'm driving. We're in traffic. We're going to get to the hotel in a few blocks—assuming this light *ever changes*—and then I've got to decide whether to self-park or go for the valet."

"Self-park so you have control of when you can get your car. Now for the compliment, what you should do is toss your hair, flash me a smile as you thank me, then carry a little warm glow of awareness wherever women carry that sort of thing."

She knew exactly where. "I don't think I've got the hair tossing quite right, yet."

"Sure you do." His voice had deepened.

"Well, thanks."

"Where's my smile?"

She bared her teeth. "I'm going to give it to the valet as we drive on through to the garage."

He laughed and Megan did feel a warm glow. Or it could have been heartburn from all the fries she'd eaten.

She turned into the hotel drive and followed a suspiciously long line of orange traffic cones. The valets couldn't need *that* many parking spaces.

"Okay, what's the plan?" she asked after she'd parked about three miles from the hotel entrance. On the positive side, the exercise would help burn off the gazillion grease calories even now making their way to her thighs.

She turned to find Barry studying her. Uh-oh.

"I need a card," he said.

This did not sound good. "Why?"

"Because I want to know what you know about Congressman Galloway that I don't."

"Oh! Oh! I've got just the card. Hang on."

Barry wasn't doing a very good job of hiding his amusement as she dug in her purse. Well, just let him laugh. "Okay, here it is. 'Do not, repeat, *do not* get into a you-scratch-my-back-and-I'll-scratch-yours situation with Barry. Specifically, do not trade information. You will always regret it.' Ha!" She waved the card at him.

He watched it like a cat watching a dangling piece of yarn, then snatched it when she got a little too close to his face.

"That was then. This is now." He tore it up.

"You don't have any information to bring to this discussion."

"I absolutely have information."

"Pure conjecture, I'll bet. You admitted that you guessed at crucial elements in your story."

"That were later proven to be correct," he pointed out.

"But out of context."

He raised his eyebrows: "I'm thinking the context has changed. How about you?"

"The only context I know is that we're sitting in my car in a remote area of the Courtland Hotel parking garage because of some sadistic valets."

He gave her the lowered-brow look—one he'd used before. "Megan." His voice was low and seductively persuasive and oh, so effective.

"Stop trying to manipulate me."

"I only want to pool our information for mutual benefit." He made it sound so logical. And sexy.

She began to imagine other poolings. "You don't know anything else." At this point, Megan was trying to convince herself. "Let's go get your rehearsal dinner story."

"Oh, I've got new stuff." He sounded so confident. So sure. So truthful. So Barry.

Megan hesitated. They'd been down this road before. But maybe this time he *did* have new information. And wasn't it her responsibility to acquire that information? She ignored the torn pieces of index card Barry had dropped into her cup holder. "Do you swear?"

"Cross my heart." He did so.

"Do you have a heart?"

He took her hand and placed it on his chest. "And it beats only for you."

He was being facetious, but she'd recently been held against that heart. It pounded steadily against her fingers, as it had beaten against her cheek. Slowly, she withdrew her hand, the texture of his shirt making her fingers tingle. Actually, it was just Barry making her tingle, and not only her fingers. "Okay," she heard herself begin. Did she really think she could resist him? "The dates on the investigation went back farther than listed on the official report."

He reached for his recorder, but Megan stilled his hand. When he nodded, indicating that he wouldn't record, she continued. "The congressman's name came up in connection with another arrest. It looked very dicey. One of the detectives wanted more info because you don't go casually throwing suspicion on a member of congress. And he didn't want to bring in the feds, either. So he looked into some stuff and then some more stuff. And weeks went by and then somebody must have tipped off Galloway because suddenly we're told he's cooperating in a sting type of investigation. But the dates we were given were well after the detective had noticed he'd begun associating with a known power player. The big guy operates out of Houston. Underlings—also pretty big—are here in Dallas. For a squeaky-clean guy, the congressman spent a lot of time with some very dirty characters. The detective—and, no, I won't reveal his name—didn't like the way his concerns were addressed. The feds came in and took all his files and told him to back off. Another detective caught the case during the cooperation phase. It just seems awfully convenient for Congressman Galloway. The first detective came to me with this after everything blew up last fall and I ended up on desk duty. There's still stuff that doesn't add up."

"Hmm."

She didn't like that hmm. "Barry, that *has* to be off the record."

"Hmm."

Megan felt icy fingers of panic claw at her. He wouldn't. But he would. He was Barry and even with the cards and his "I'm going to show you the inner me" promises, she'd once again been fooled. "So what do you know?" He'd better know something. He'd better.

Barry had been staring off into space. He turned to her. "Congressman Galloway doesn't have a sister."

Megan waited, but he didn't say anything else. "That's it? That's your big piece of information?"

"He lied, Megan. He told the police at his hotel room that his sister's suitcase had also been trashed. They were waiting until she arrived to find out if anything was missing. He doesn't have a sister."

"Maybe he meant sister-in-law."

"He doesn't have one of those, either."

"Well, so what?" Megan was suddenly angry. "I just told you information that no one outside the department knows and your big news is that the congressman doesn't have a sister. That is not on par. I need more."

Barry went still and she knew he wasn't thinking about the congressman. "So do I," he murmured in a husky, gravelly voice that changed everything.

They stared at each other, the silence thickening, the mood changing. The tension was still between them, but it was a different tension. She should say something to break it because this was just Barry's way of distracting her. She should open the car door. She should not watch Barry's eyes take on a slumberous and decidedly predatory expression. She really shouldn't encourage the unfurling sensation in the pit of her stomach.

And she should tell the voice yelling, "Kiss me already!" to be quiet. She was just about to, truly she was, when Barry leaned toward her, skimmed his hand around her cheek to the back of her neck, hauled her to him, and kissed her. Hard.

And she kissed him back. Equally hard.

Megan didn't know what that was supposed to

prove and frankly, didn't care. The kiss was that good. Or bad, as the case might be.

Hands on either side of her face, Barry held her firmly against his mouth. Megan did love a man who took charge and Barry was definitely in charge.

In fact, for all the great technique and practiced smoothness of the last kiss, Megan liked this one better, even with the gearbox and bucket seats in the way. Although, it would be great to have an unobstructed kiss, for once. Or twice. But this kiss held a rawness that excited her. This kiss was because he couldn't *not* kiss her. He wanted her.

And she wanted him, too.

Barry was usually so affable and charming that she didn't think he had a kiss like this in him. Words like *raw* and *primitive* and *plundering* were not Barry words. Or at least they hadn't been. They sure were now.

And those tongue moves that made her go boneless before? They were back. Oh, yeah. So she let him know she had a few moves of her own. Drawing his tongue deeply inside her mouth, she moaned, allowing him to feel the vibrations. Then she stroked its length.

His hands clutched at her before dropping to her shoulders and back as he tried to draw her closer. But there was nowhere to go. The bucket seats were in the way and it was probably a good thing. A kiss like this one didn't stay just a kiss for long.

And it didn't. Maybe because their hands had been tied last time, they went a little overboard this time. Megan slipped her arms beneath Barry's jacket and ran her hands over his back, feeling the muscles and the bumps of his spine, measuring the breadth of his shoulders and the narrowness of his waist.

Barry kept one hand cupped around the back of her neck as his other splayed against her lower back in a commanding way that she liked in spite of herself. When he lowered his hand to slip it beneath her hips and wedge her closer, she forgot about whether she should or shouldn't like what he was doing and just went with it.

Going with it meant she reached down and grabbed his butt. He gave a surprised groan and inhaled deeply as he yanked the hem of her T-shirt from her jeans.

His fingers caressed the slice of midriff before heading northward, northward toward the land of no return.

Megan ached for his touch. She craved it. She craved him. It didn't matter where, or when, or for how long. And as his fingers skimmed the tight elastic band of her jogging bra, she realized she didn't care what the consequences would be. Except she *should* care.

And that's when Megan pulled back, literally wrenching her mouth from his. They stared at each other, both gulping for air.

"You can't kiss somebody like that unless you really mean it!" Megan said when she could speak.

"How could I not mean it?" Barry looked like someone who'd been awakened from a sound sleep—or interrupted from a kiss he was really into.

"You could be trying to seduce me into going back to the congressman's room instead of the rehearsal dinner."

where Megan had been doing an excellent statue imitation behind the flowers.

As soon as their eyes met, she rolled hers and slipped down the hall well in advance of Sally and her bridesmaids.

Barry grinned. What a woman. He sat on the bench she'd recently vacated and laced his fingers behind his head.

So SHE WAS REDUCED to hiding out in restroom stalls.

Megan was more bemused than anything. If she considered this in a different way, her evening with Barry was actually a pretty good date. She could call it a date, couldn't she? They'd kissed. Two goose bump–raising times. He'd bought her dinner. Sounded like a date to her.

She was getting a handle on what made Barry tick and was more than relieved to discover that some of the things he'd done in the past were out of utter cluelessness and not malice. He didn't mean to hurt people—or her—he'd simply never got feedback before. So she was giving him feedback and, wonder of wonders, he actually seemed to be learning something.

She didn't delude herself about him—well, not much. Barry would be ruthless when it was required.

Could she?

If she doubted herself after kissing him, what would happen after she slept with him?

Megan half listened to Sally whine and her bridesmaids commiserate and thought about what it would be like when she and Barry had their former jobs back.

Would he treat her differently? Go easier on her? Would he expect special treatment? Inside information?

No to all of the above. Megan grinned. Did she want it any other way?

The bridesmaids were talking about makeup sex when they all went out the door. Megan would have liked to hear the end of that conversation, but it was not to be. After she was sure there were no stragglers, she got an index card out of her purse and went to find Barry.

"Anything?" he asked.

She sat beside him on the bench and handed him the card.

"That good?" He read the card. "I remember this. You were being tight-lipped that day."

"And you were a jerk. Following me to my car to verify a quote and then yelling that I knew something else. The other reporters came running. It was like blood in shark-infested waters. I did *not* know anything else and the next day the stories were all, 'Police-department spokeswoman Megan Esterbrook refused comment.'"

"Well, you did."

"But I didn't know anything else to comment on! That's different than refusing. Refusing sounds like I could have but chose not to. There's a difference and I came off like I was hiding something. That was really bad of you."

He looked at her, unsmiling. "Do you want an apology?"

"Don't you think I deserve one?"

"My responsibility is to print the truth. I took a

chance that you did know more. That time I was wrong."

"That doesn't sound like an apology."

"It's not. Because I know you've concealed information when the press didn't ask the right questions."

True. Megan took back the card and tore it up herself.

"So what do you know?" Barry asked.

"Makeup sex is supposed to be really good." She watched him swallow and smothered a grin. "Gus has got some serious groveling before the makeup part, though."

"Anything else?"

"They aren't going to name their first child after Derek. In fact, he might not even make the Christmas-card list. Sally's seriously ticked at him. Figures he's responsible for Gus not being there."

"She's right. Does she know anything about Gus's former profession?"

Megan thought. "I don't think she's as stupid as people assume. My guess is that she is aware of whatever he did in the past, but doesn't want to know the details." Megan snickered. "It's not like she doesn't have some details of her own to hide."

Barry leaned his head back against the wall. "In other words, you didn't hear anything useful."

Megan thought the sex tip was useful. "Not really," she said with elaborate casualness and leaned her head against the wall, too. "Just some blathering about Derek neglecting his best-man duties and spending all his time with the congressman who was going on and on about his hotel room being ransacked and that he wanted Derek to watch his Dallas office in case it got hit. Sally felt that was the police's job and that Derek's job was to give the bachelor party."

"So there is a connection." Barry whistled. "All right, Megan!" He high-fived her. "Guess where we're going?"

Megan didn't have to guess. "The bachelor party?"

"What a sense of humor. Let's go."

MEGAN KNEW THEY WERE GOING to Congressman Galloway's campaign office but she made Barry take a card anyway.

There were only a couple of cards left. They were huge issues to her and she wasn't going to surrender them lightly.

The cards had been her defense against Barry, the layers protecting her heart. As he peeled them away one by one, he'd also discarded his own protective layers. Megan hadn't expected that. She found that even when she disagreed with Barry, she liked him. She'd never anticipated getting to know him and never thought he'd want to know her.

She was either headed for the real thing, or she was going to get seriously hurt. Maybe both.

"Slow down. There it is." Barry pointed. Megan dutifully slowed the car as they passed the dark building housing the congressman's local office and, when it was an election year, his campaign headquarters.

Stakeouts hadn't exactly been her favorite thing

when she'd been a rookie, but she'd never been on a stakeout with Barry.

"First of all, before we get to the fun stuff, let me show you why we're here," he said.

"There's fun stuff?"

"Absolutely."

They'd parked her car in a Kwiky Mart across the street and down the block from the congressman's office. It was located in the north part of Dallas, near Richardson, in a lushly landscaped strip mall, which was an oxymoron, but Megan knew they could use the lush landscaping to their advantage when the time came. Unfortunately, there was a brightly lit gas station on the corner, so approaching the office's lush landscaping undetected was iffy.

She'd worry about that later. "What fun stuff?"

Barry opened his computer and Megan suppressed a sigh. She'd been hoping for a different kind of fun stuff. But how to change the mood? Right now, it was comfortable and friendly. And make no mistake, she liked that. A lot. But keeping things comfortable and friendly was hard when all the time she was fighting the urge for more. She wanted to touch him. Anywhere would do for now.

She wasn't averse to making the first move, as long as she knew it was welcome. And that was the problem. Barry was very carefully avoiding eye contact of any duration and certainly all physical contact. Earlier, she'd enjoyed his hand on the small of her back. What had happened to that? He held himself away from her. Was he avoiding her?

Honestly, if she weren't wearing a gray hoodie and jeans, she'd bet he wouldn't avoid her.

"So what fun stuff on the computer am I going to see?" Even to herself she sounded grumpy.

Barry turned the screen around. "From the employee-only archives of the *Dallas Press*. Behold. Congressman Galloway's sister."

Megan stared at what the retail trade called a plus-size woman emerging from what appeared to be a town house with a wrought-iron fence. She was walking a small dog. Megan didn't know what kind. "You said he didn't have a sister."

"I don't think he does, but that's who we were told she was. I see a family resemblance. Don't you?"

"Unfortunately for her, yes. Where was this taken?"

"Georgetown, in front of his town house. When it looked like I had something on him last year, the paper sent a photographer and me to Washington D.C."

Megan didn't get it. "Okay, so who is this woman really?"

Barry showed her another picture. And another. And another. In the last one, a breeze lifted the hemline of the print button-down dress.

"If I had calves and knees like that, I'd shoot myself," Megan said.

Wearing a weird smile, Barry leaned back against the car door. "My calves and knees look kinda like that."

"Yeah, but you're a ma—" She gasped as understanding dawned. "No!"

"I'm thinkin' yes."

"You think that's Galloway? No way!"

"It fits. First of all, the congressman and his sister have never appeared together and she's never been interviewed, alluded to, or present at any of his inaugurations. She's not mentioned in his official bio."

"Then wouldn't he be taking a chance by mentioning her if she didn't exist?" Megan was still grappling with the idea of Congressman Galloway as a cross-dresser.

"He panicked."

"What about in Washington?"

"Maybe he panicked there, too, and got away with it. Who knows? But here's what I think. He's on the House Armed Services Committee and there's an important vote coming up on Monday. Most cross-dressers find wearing the clothes of the opposite sex reduces stress and gives them a certain control. Remember how agitated Galloway was? My guess is that he'd planned to go out this weekend and now is afraid to. And you know what else? I think he's being blackmailed for it."

Not again. "That's what you thought last year."

"And that's what I think now."

"That kind of thinking got us into all kinds of trouble last year." Megan sat back and considered everything. Much as she hated to admit it, Barry's theory fit. Of course it fit last time, too. "When did you figure all this out?"

"A lot of it came together while we were eating dinner."

"You mean while you were on the Internet and I was stealing your French fries?"

He nodded.

"Wow." Though the fries had been good, she clearly hadn't made the best use of her time.

"Now see? Isn't this fun?"

"Fun might not be the word I'd use."

Barry's smile faded. "Yeah, I know. I don't like the sense of urgency I picked up from Derek and Gus. What was so important that Derek had to ask his buddy—retired from all accounts—to miss all his wedding hoopla? And I don't like the abject fear I saw on Galloway's face at the rehearsal dinner. This goes deeper than political embarrassment."

"He *is* on one of the most powerful congressional committees," Megan pointed out. "If he's cross-dressing, people will laugh at him. He won't be effective and he'll lose power. That's enough to make him panic."

"Maybe." Barry stared out the car window.

He thought it had to do with the upcoming vote, but Megan didn't want to talk about it. She felt strangely detached. Last year, she would have been on the phone to her supervisor, her heart in her throat. This year…this year, she understood that she'd been a scapegoat. This year, she was more cautious.

A yawn caught her by surprise and she checked her watch. Nearly midnight. "So what do you think is going to happen here?"

"I have no idea, but I'd love to get inside that office."

She knew he did and she'd known it ever since they'd arrived. If she weren't here, she suspected that Barry would try to break in, but he hadn't asked her to help him or look the other way while he broke in because he knew she wouldn't.

He'd learned that about her. Megan smiled to herself. A trainable man was so incredibly sexy, she could hardly stand it. She was tempted to break in just to reward him.

However, it was late. To keep herself awake, she asked him where he lived.

"I live just north of here in Richardson in a town house," he answered. "How about you?"

"Last year, I moved into a rental house in a modest area of Dallas, as they say. I have an option to buy at the end of the year. I like it. It's an older neighborhood and mowing the lawn is a great stress reliever." She was talking about lawn maintenance. She couldn't believe she was sitting inches away from Barry and talking about her yard.

"Not for me," Barry said. "I don't have time for yard work."

"So how do you relax?" she asked.

"I don't need to relax."

"Barry, everybody needs downtime to stay sane."

He drew a deep breath. "Downtime makes me tense."

Megan shook her head. "You can't work all the time."

"I've been known to watch TV," he offered.

"Probably checking out the competition."

"I can't help it." He shifted and pulled out his computer. "I'm going to interview you. A feature about the police-department spokeswoman is long overdue."

"Oh, please." What a transparent ploy to avoid talking about himself.

"Humor me."

"And it's *former* police-department spokeswoman."

"Merely a temporary career detour."

She smiled at his optimism, which he rightly took as a sign of weakening.

"It'll help you stay awake."

He'd caught her in another yawn.

There were things Megan would rather do than talk about herself, but the next hour passed quickly and she shot a few questions Barry's way, too.

They were a lot alike for two people who were so different. Both had experienced normal childhoods with normal families, yet Megan had emerged as a straight arrow who followed the rules with loyalty and responsibility, and Barry had become suspiciously cynical of rules and people.

They were actually good for each other and Megan wondered if Barry realized it. From Barry, Megan had learned to question. She hoped he'd learned to trust from her. Okay, trust some. Just a little. Just once, maybe, to try it out.

She talked about everything from playing soccer and running track to her favorite Christmas present—extravagantly expensive track shoes filled with makeup.

"Wasn't that a mixed message?" Barry asked.

Megan grinned. "It was an *embracing* message. And the makeup was waterproof and had sunscreen in it. Sports makeup!"

"Okay. Boyfriends."

"What do you mean, 'okay, boyfriends'?"

"Did you have any?"

"Yes."

"And?"

And she'd never felt anything like what she felt for Barry. Her boyfriends had been...pleasant. She'd kept waiting to feel more and never had. But with Barry...with Barry, she felt too much.

"Okay. No comment on the boyfriends."

"Let's just say that my body may have been touched but my heart hasn't been." *Unlike now,* she wanted to add, *when my heart's been touched and my body hasn't been. Or not much, anyway.*

And it wasn't going to be in the near future, if what she saw over Barry's shoulder was any indication. "I don't believe it. There's somebody lurking around the office."

Barry whipped his head around. "Told ya. Come on."

"Come on where?"

"Out of the car—your side. We can get closer while he's occupied with breaking in."

Yet another huge assumption on Barry's part, but moments later, Megan found herself squatting behind her car anyway.

"Barry, it could be a worker with a legitimate reason for being there."

"After midnight?"

"Not unheard of."

"Do you really believe that?"

"Well, I would, except for the sneaking-around-the-back part." She pointed.

"Let's go." They skulked across the street. Barry excelled at skulking, which didn't surprise Megan a bit. What did surprise her was the spurt of adrenaline she felt. She liked skulking. She could really get into skulking.

They crouched in the bushes—pittosporum—and peered through the front windows. There was a bobbing glow, obviously from a flashlight, and then someone closed the blinds.

"Do you think this qualifies as suspicious activity? Suspicious enough for an off-duty policewoman to investigate?" Barry whispered.

Megan hesitated. The glow behind the blinds was brighter, bright enough to silhouette a person.

And then two persons.

"Hey," Barry said softly. "Who's that? Where did he come from?"

"Okay, I'm calling this in. I'm on desk duty so I can't go in by myself and you don't count." She reached for her cell phone before remembering that she didn't have one anymore. "I've got to go back to the store and use their phone. Do not, repeat, do not leave this spot."

Silence.

"Barry?"

"Card."

"No. This is beyond a card. Promise me you will not go into the office."

He gazed down at her. "How about if I promise to use my best judgment?"

Megan would have argued, but the second person looked like he or she was getting strangled. Or it could be a couple of workers back for some after-hours fun. Arms and shadows...clothing being removed? She listened intently. There were no sounds of struggle—no sounds period.

"It's not breaking and entering if the door is unlocked," Barry murmured.

"That is not exactly true." She turned and looked him full in the face.

He looked back. "So how many cards do you have left?"

"Two."

He held out his hand. She should run for the Kwiky Mart. She should not play cards with Barry.

But one of the cards left was the biggie—the one that had landed her on desk duty. Maybe guilt would keep him from going into the office while she made the call. Silently, she handed it to him.

Barry read it, then gazed at her. "I'm sorry." It was all he said, but he pocketed the card without tearing it up.

This was supposed to be the big showdown between them, but Megan discovered his simple apology was enough. It had happened. They were past it. Time to move on. Nodding, she took off for the convenience store.

A patrol car was only one exit away on the freeway, and arrived quickly and silently, which was good, but with its lights flashing, which was bad. Hadn't she said *in progress?*

Megan hadn't even made it back across the street before she saw a black-clad figure slip between the buildings. Oh, great. Just great.

But why hadn't he just gone out the back and escaped down the alley behind the buildings? It was almost as though he wanted to get caught, or make sure they knew he'd been there. She thought about that only after she'd waved the patrol car after him. Moments later, a second patrol car sped past.

Megan looked over to the pittosporum, knowing Barry was no longer there. Knowing that he was using the momentary absence of the police to sneak inside the campaign headquarters.

Still she went over to the bushes. "Barry?"

No answer. "Barry!"

He'd promised. No, wait. Actually, he hadn't promised. He'd said he'd use his best judgment.

Megan stared at the closed blinds. If she stayed out here, all she had were suspicions, suspicions she had no intention of sharing. On the other hand, he was in there contaminating a crime scene. She drew a deep breath and gazed skyward at the few stars shining through the city lights.

All right. Okay. *Fine.* She was going to say three hell Barrys and go in after him.

9

BARRY WAS NOT ALONE. He eyed the other person in Congressman Galloway's office and tried to figure out what to do.

"Ma'am... What's that? Call you Dawn? Well, Dawn, if you ask me, you've gone a little heavy on the lipstick." And then he punched her.

That would be the moment Megan arrived.

"Omigawd! *Barry!*"

"Hi, Megan. Where are your friends?" He waved her over as Dawn popped back up and wobbled around a bit, her hat and wig askew. Barry straightened them and exhaled.

"Two patrol cars are pursuing the perp." Megan stood beside him and stared at the plastic blow-up doll. "This is the other person—thing we saw?"

"Megan, meet Dawn. Dawn, this is Megan. She'll be your police officer for the evening." Barry enjoyed watching Megan's mouth open and close. He had fond memories of that mouth.

"So—so our burglar brought something in instead of taking something out?" she asked.

"It appears so."

Megan shook her head. "This is wrong on so many levels."

"More levels than you know. Check under the dress."

Megan lifted the hemline, her eyes widened and then she laughed. "That's impressive."

"Nothing special."

Megan ignored him. "Okay, Barry. Why is a life-size, anatomically *enhanced* male sex doll dressed in women's clothing in Congressman Donald Galloway's office?"

Barry peeled off a paper name tag that read Hi! I'm Dawn.

"Stop tampering with evidence!"

"Evidence of what? I assume you made the Dawn/Don/Donald connection."

"Yeah." She pressed her fingers to her temples. "Okay, so somebody knows he cross-dresses and…this is blackmail?"

Barry stared at the doll. "It's a little tenuous. Maybe this is to scare him. Or start some rumors."

"Or maybe it's a joke?"

"Ha-ha."

Megan cased the perimeter of the room. "Did you touch anything else?"

"No. But I'd like to."

She shot a glance at him.

This was going to be tricky. "I'd like to ruffle a few files, deflate Dawn, here, and take her away."

Horror crossed her face as he'd known it would. "But that's compromising a crime scene!"

"No, here's a compromise—I'll leave the files alone and deflate Dawn."

"Why?"

"Because, Megan, following the rules in this case would be bad."

He could see her struggle to grasp something that was pretty much against all her beliefs. "I'm not saying we suppress evidence—I'm saying we choose who sees it. This isn't about a simple break-in. This is the kind of thing we show Gus and Derek and your supervisor's supervisor. Not the patrol cops and the night-beat reporters."

She stared at him, clearly torn.

"Think."

"I think you'll parlay this into an exclusive story."

"Okay, don't think. Let's go with trust."

"You're the one who needs to learn trust."

"I have! Why do you think I'm giving the congressman a break? I said I'd show Dawn to Derek and Gus—and your bigwigs. I'm trusting people all over the place."

Blue-and-red lights pulsed against the closed blinds. The police were back.

"Megan? It's decision time."

Megan gazed at the flickering lights. "Well, hell, Barry," she said.

They stared at each other and then she grimaced. "I'll stall them. Take Dawn and get out of here."

"I love you." And he meant it.

"No, you don't." She got out her badge and opened the door. "Corrupting people just turns you on."

"That, too." But she was already gone.

Barry grinned. What a trooper. He couldn't believe it. Megan, the little rule-follower, was stretching, if not outright breaking the rules. How sexy was that? Maybe corruption did turn him on.

Barry grabbed the Dawn doll and pulled at the inflating tab. It had a leak guard and he didn't have time to pinch it and wait for the thing to deflate.

Looking around he found a pair of scissors in a desk caddy, grabbed them and stabbed the doll, trying not to think of Galloway as he did so. Squeezing the plastic against him, he crumpled the doll, clothes and all, and eased out the back door into the service alley. Once outside, he listened carefully, hearing the murmur of voices from the street. Megan and the cops. After he ditched Dawn, should he hide or show himself? He and Megan should have coordinated stories.

The voices grew louder. They were going inside the office. Barry decided to sneak the long way around the back of the connected buildings of the strip mall. When he reached the end of the alley, he stashed Dawn in a Dumpster, then crept past the fronts of the other businesses until he was close to where he and Megan had hidden in the bushes before.

He saw Megan standing outside the front door of Galloway's office, looking for Barry without trying to show it. She eased sideways in his direction, but before he could signal her, another police cruiser arrived and she went out to the curb to meet it.

Her hair gleamed in the moonlight as did the T-shirt beneath her hoodie. She gestured, then stuck a thumb in the front pocket of her jeans and Barry grinned to see such a male stance with that hair and that chest.

But that was the quintessential Megan. Watching her direct the cops in the moonlight and covering for him…she'd never looked sexier in her life.

He was corrupted. Totally and completely corrupted. And he was going to take her down with him.

He stooped and felt around for something to throw. All he could find was a chunk of pine-bark mulch in the bedding, so he tossed that onto the sidewalk.

Then he tossed another.

Megan didn't notice until the fifth brown piece landed on the sidewalk. She backed toward him and when she got within grabbing distance, he grabbed, pulling her smack up against him and into the bushes.

"You feel so good." He buried his face into the side of her neck and breathed in.

"Oh, *Barry*," she moaned.

Hello? A moan? Already? He raised his head. "Miss me?"

"I feel so alive! I've broken rules…and I *like* it!" She shivered against him. "The adrenaline—my heart is pounding and all my nerves are hyperaware—this is what you feel too, isn't it?"

"I get a buzz, yeah."

She turned in his arms, which caused a buzz of a different kind. "This is so much more than a buzz! I feel hot. So, so hot." She wrapped her arms around his neck and planted a quick, hard kiss on his open mouth as she ran her hands over his chest. "Why didn't you tell me it was like this?"

Barry was dealing with his own heat issues. "Who knew you'd take to corruption?" He bent to kiss her again.

But Megan pulled back as though they'd been doused with cold water. "We're doing the right thing, aren't we? I mean, the wrong thing for the right reason?"

Ah, man, he'd killed her buzz. "Yes. The right thing. Absolutely." But she still looked uncertain. Why couldn't he have kept his mouth shut? He tried to get back to the kissing, but she pulled away.

"They'll be looking for me."

"*I'll* be looking for you." He reached for her.

Megan held him off and glanced behind her. "Somebody is going to notice that I'm not waiting by the cars. Where's Dawn?"

"Megan, forget about Dawn. You can't kiss a guy like that and walk away."

"Hey!" She snapped her fingers in front of his face. "What do you think is going to happen here in the bushes?"

"I—"

"I realize it's hard for you to think right now—no pun intended—so I'm thinking for both of us. Concentrate. Where's the doll?"

Barry dropped his arms, aware that, though they were in the bushes, he'd still blown an opportunity. He concentrated, overly aware of her scent, the way she'd felt in his arms, and the taste of her mouth. This was not what he should be concentrating on.

Her face softened. "Barry, don't look at me that way." She barely mouthed the words.

"You're looking at me the same way."

"I know."

He could reach out and touch her and she'd be his.

And hate him afterward. "Okay." Filling his lungs with the night air, he clenched his hands. "The doll is in a Dumpster. Give me your keys and I'll stash her in your trunk."

"I don't want her—it—in my trunk."

"Do you want them to find her when they search the alley?"

"You're right." Grimacing, Megan pulled the keys out of her pocket. "Don't let them see you."

"I'm a shadow in the night," he vowed. "What did you tell them about why you were here, anyway?"

"Oh, you know…."

"No."

"I said that you live around here and I was giving you a ride home after you had car trouble. I stopped at the Kwiky Mart and saw suspicious activity at the campaign headquarters."

"Very good. It's always best to tell the truth when you're lying."

"That's so profound and yet, so wrong." She reached up and pinched his cheek. "Go stash Dawn. I'll head off the guys."

"I love it when you talk dirty."

Megan grinned and slipped through the bushes.

THE PATROLMEN WERE COMING OUT of the congressman's office just as Megan reached the spot by their car where she'd been waiting.

Cutting it so close gave her another shot of adrenaline.

Her actions alternately thrilled and appalled her. And turned her on. Barry knew that and she figured it could be a good thing. Also making him wait was a good thing. After all, how long had she waited, hoping that he'd notice her and afraid that he would?

"Can't tell if anything was taken," one of the officers was saying as the other two got into their car and drove off. "We're sealing this puppy. Thanks for sticking around, Megan. We'll take it from here."

It was a clear dismissal. Time for her to go. Had Barry had enough time to stash the doll? If she started walking toward her car in the Kwiky Mart lot, then she'd draw attention to it and what if Barry was just now stuffing the blow-up doll into her trunk?

Her heart pounded as she nodded to her fellow officers of the law, avoided thinking about what she was doing to that same law, and tried to stop an outbreak of nervous giggling. She waved inanely, a huge gesture so Barry could see it if he was looking her way, and know she had no choice but to leave.

One of the guys, the younger one, waved back, a goofy sort of grin on his face.

"Blond getting to your brain, Esterbrook?" said his partner.

She struck a pose that came from who-knew-where, flipped her hair, and slowly turned.

They obliged with a whistle, but more importantly, Megan was able to see her car and no Barry.

She'd just vamped. She'd never vamped anyone in her life. She didn't know how to vamp—or she hadn't. But the situation had called for it and her adrenaline-heightened state had provided the very skill she'd needed.

Without turning back to look, Megan knew the

patrolmen hadn't left the scene and she still hadn't heard their car start up by the time she reached hers. Great. What now? She could stall by going inside the Kwiky Mart. She'd do that.

After wandering the aisles long enough to make the lone clerk nervous, she was withdrawing a bottle of water from the cooler when the two patrolmen came in.

Oh, great. Just great. Megan nodded at them and joined them at the checkout counter at the same time she remembered that her purse was locked in the glove compartment of her car. And what did she have to pay with? In her pocket, she had the hundred-dollar bills Gus had given her. What convenience store clerk would take a hundred at this hour?

One of the guys unknowingly rescued her. "Hey, I'll get that for you."

"Thanks." It was skating so close to the edge of discovery that kept her on a perpetual adrenaline high. Perpetual adrenaline highs were also exhausting.

Megan made idle chitchat with them while they bought coffee and her water, and then everybody walked outside together.

"So, Megan." The younger of the two, the one who'd paid for her water, cleared his throat. "You seein' anybody?"

He was hitting on her. Never again would she doubt the power of blond highlights. "Um, yeah, kind of." She reached for her keys before remembering that she didn't have her keys, and why. This could be bad.

"It's Sutton, right?" Both snickered.

Megan was unnerved before remembering that

her antagonism toward Barry was well-known. "Yeah, right."

Turning toward her car, she relaxed briefly— briefly because at that very moment, through the window, Megan saw Barry hiding on the floor of her car. And if she could see him, so could the patrolmen. And how would she explain that?

"But you *are* seeing somebody," the young guy persisted.

"Kind of," she repeated a little shrilly. *Leave, already*.

"Yeah, I figured."

He did? When? When did he figure? And why?

Hands on hips, looking down, the rookie did everything but stub his toe in the dirt. "Well, lemme know if, you know, things don't work out."

"Sure," Megan chirped, conscious that his partner was about to bust a gut trying to keep from laughing.

Megan sent him a don't-be-a-jerk look and pulled at the driver's-side door. To her immense relief, it opened.

"Hey—you didn't lock your car?" Incredulity sounded in the rookie's voice and rightly so.

She didn't have her keys, either. Barry had her keys. The Barry who was hidden in her car. She flipped her hair. What the heck. It had worked as a distraction a few minutes ago. "Usually I do, but I started to drive off and decided at the last minute that I was thirsty." She raised the bottle of water and gave them a silly-me smile.

There were no answering smiles. They weren't buying it. "You left your car unlocked at a stop-and-rob at two in the morning." Both men shook their heads. "Not so slick, Esterbrook."

"Check your car before you get in." The older, experienced cop wore a stern look and Megan *knew* she was going to hear about this on Monday.

She dutifully looked in her car. Barry gave her a toothy fake smile, which made her want to laugh in spite of everything. "All clear!" she sang to the men and tried to climb in without letting them see the inside.

She knew they'd wait until her car started, so she flung out her hand for Barry to give her the keys, hoping the men wouldn't notice that she'd left her purse in the car, too. She was lucky that Barry had unlocked the car or she would have had them offering to pop the lock for her.

After starting the car, she lowered the window. "Thanks!" She waved. They waved back. She smiled inanely and spoke through gritted teeth. "I'm going to have to drive off."

"So drive," Barry whispered.

"Hey, Megan," the rookie called out. "When you realize that guy isn't enough for you and you're ready for a real man, I'm here."

His partner cracked up.

"I'll keep you in mind." As she backed up her car, Megan supposed it was too much to hope that Barry hadn't heard that.

A hand stroked her calf. "I wonder what guy he's talking about." His hand inched higher.

The car jerked. "I'm trying to drive here. They're following right behind me."

"Mmm. Danger. The thrill of possible discovery." His hand crept toward her thigh.

"You keep your thrills to yourself."

"You don't mean that."

"I mean it when I'm driving."

"Stop driving."

Megan glanced in the rearview mirror. "They'll stop, too."

"So turn."

Glancing at the congressman's headquarters as she drove past, Megan turned. The patrol car's lights began flashing.

"Oh, great."

"What? Did you forget to signal?"

"I signaled!" Heart pounding so hard it made her hands shake, Megan slowed and then stopped at the side of the street. The guys were just fooling around, but when they pulled up beside her car, there was no way they'd miss seeing Barry.

But with a beep of the horn, the patrol car zoomed around her and headed on into the night.

After staring at the rapidly receding taillights, Megan thudded her head on the steering wheel and exhaled in a *whoosh*. "They're gone. They got a call."

BARRY TOOK A MOMENT to savor the relief. "Got a good buzz off that one."

Poor Megan looked like she was about to come unglued.

Barry exhaled. "All clear?"

She checked the empty street and nodded.

"You okay?" Barry unfolded himself and got into the passenger seat.

"I've hit my thrill limit," Megan said. "When I

looked in the car and saw you hiding on the floor, I nearly had a heart attack."

Barry massaged his calf muscles. "I had no place else to go. I wasn't expecting them to come to the store."

"I know. I think the clerk probably pressed a panic button because I hung around there for so long."

She leaned back against the headrest, her throat white in the moonlight. Barry stared at her, feeling desire well up until it nearly rendered him senseless. Who knew he was a neck man?

"If I were a vampire, I'd find you irresistible right about now." He traced his finger down her throat and over to where her pulse beat steadily. Slower than his.

She turned her head, blinked, and said, "So bite me."

Oh, this could be good. "Left my fangs in my other coat." He turned to his side so they were face-to-face.

"Pity," she whispered softly.

His head pounded. They should go back to the hotel to get the congressman's reaction to the break-in. That's what they should do. By now the police would have notified him. And Barry would have bet a month's pay that Derek and maybe even Gus, the groom, would have been somewhere around. A perfect opportunity to introduce them to Dawn.

It would be the story of a lifetime.

And he wasn't going to write it because he was more interested in the story sitting across from him. "About the congressman's office…"

Disappointment flashed in her eyes and he smiled.

"What about it?" she asked.

"Who knows if the guy who broke in will come back? Someone should keep watch."

It took her a second and then she smiled, too. "Sounds logical."

He shifted forward. "This isn't really the best spot for surveillance."

She shifted forward, too. "Any suggestions?"

"Remember the black leather couch in the reception area?"

"I guess so."

He smiled.

She gasped softly. "You're kidding. You aren't suggesting that we…we break in?"

"Yes."

"And ignore the crime-scene tape?"

"Yes."

"And just…sit on the couch?"

"No."

"No?" Her voice grew husky. "I can't think of anything else we could do, unless you're interested in having hot, sweaty sex on the couch?"

His breath hissed between his teeth. "I was thinking of making love on the couch, but hot, sweaty sex certainly works for me."

She closed her eyes.

He couldn't tell if that was a good thing or a bad thing. As the silence lengthened, he was thinking it wasn't so good. One of them should say something before the other exploded with anxiety. "You've got a card left."

"Doesn't matter."

"Give me the card."

She shook her head and started the car.

He'd thought... Had he read her wrong? Was she rejecting him? What could be on that card?

Her purse was still in the glove compartment. He popped it open.

Megan started driving as Barry fished for the card. She executed a sharp turn, then slammed on the brakes as Barry plucked the card out of her purse.

They were at the alley entry to the congressman's office.

And then he read the card. There were only two words. "Give in?"

"Yes."

"Give in to...anything in particular?"

She smiled a smile full of promise. "I like to keep my options open."

He smiled back. "I do like the way you think. I did some thinking, myself, back at the Kwiky Mart." He showed her the package in his jacket pocket.

"And that answers that question. There's only one more." She leaned toward him until her lips were a breath away from his. "How fast can you get us into that building?"

Pretty damn fast, but Barry wasn't sure he should own up to that. "It shouldn't be too difficult." And they clambered out of the car and stood in front of the crime-scene-wrapped door.

First rule of breaking and entering—check to see if the door is unlocked. Barry turned the knob. It was locked.

Here was a tricky part. Barry fingered the lock-pick knife on his key chain. "Megan, why don't you go around front and see if anyone is there?"

"Why?"

"How to put this…"

"Come on, Barry. If we're caught, we're caught. Can you actually picture me whining, 'But I don't know *how* he opened the door'?"

But she was the police and he was, well… "At least turn around."

Shaking her head in amusement, Megan turned her back.

Barry removed his keys, pried the tension wrench out of the top of the knife and opened the picks.

It was dark, and the keys were jangling and lust was making his hands shake while desire clouded his vision. Or it could have been the other way around. He was not at his lock-picking best.

"Barry." Megan shifted her purse to her left shoulder and held out her hand. "Give me the tension wrench."

Silently he gave it to her. Megan examined the pick elements fanning out of the knife, selected a different one and moments later, opened the door.

She returned his keys. "Don't make this into an ego thing. I was trained."

"It's not an ego thing—"

Megan interrupted him with a kiss. Barry clamped his arms around her and kissed her back to show her that his ego could stand women who took the initiative, too.

Lights from a passing car shone through the binds, sending stripes of light traveling over the floor.

Megan flinched and Barry pulled back just far enough to rest his forehead on hers. "We don't have to do this, if you don't want to."

"Are you kidding? I just got another shot of adrenaline. Let's get to the couch before the tingles wear off."

"Oh, honey. Those aren't tingles. *I'll* show you tingles." And he kissed her all the way to the leather couch.

The fact that she enthusiastically kissed him back hampered their progress, but made the journey a lot more fun. When they got to the back of the couch Megan, giggling wickedly, tipped them over, landing on top of Barry.

All in all, it was a great place to be.

Megan stretched out on top of him and licked his jaw as she moved—no, *undulated* against him. *Now*, he was free to enjoy. Quite possibly, he'd never felt anything so wonderful in his life. He quit breathing, afraid she might stop.

But she stopped anyway and patted his jacket pockets. "Your clothes are too lumpy and there are too many of them."

She straddled him and Barry struggled to sit up. "This is not an incurable problem."

He shrugged off his jacket and prepared to drop it over the back, but Megan stopped him. "Keep those condoms within reach."

"Good thinking." How could she think? He couldn't think. And didn't even miss thinking. He dropped the jacket in a puddle on the floor.

"These—" Megan slipped off his shoes "—we can toss." She handed them to him and untied her cross trainers. Without looking, she tossed them over her shoulders. One landed on a desk and knocked over a plastic mug filled with pencils. The other crashed into her purse and tipped it over onto the floor.

Barry's first toss over his shoulders landed in a trash can. "Don't let me forget that shoe." The second bounced and scooted beneath a standing display of political literature.

Megan whipped off her hoodie, leaving an impressively packed white T-shirt. The realization that he was shortly going to see what was packing that shirt rendered Barry mute.

Megan leaned forward, her fingers working the buttons of his shirt. "For a guy who talks all the time, you sure don't say much."

"I'm afraid this is a dream and if I say anything, I'll wake up. Or you'll stop."

She sat back. "That is so sweet."

"See? You stopped."

"Only because your cuffs are still buttoned and, while I could get into ripping, I know your wrists are sore."

Involuntarily, he glanced at hers. In the ambient light, it looked as though she wore two dark bracelets.

Megan held them up. "Not sexy." She pointed to his bare chest. "Sexy. Now take off your shirt."

"Aren't you going to take—" *Off yours,* he was going to say, but Megan was ahead of him. Crossing her arms, she yanked her T-shirt over her head, revealing an impressively upholstered chest.

Barry tossed his shirt over the back of the couch as he surveyed the fortress before him much as a knight of old cased a castle. This was no wisp of lace with a front catch that would spring loose with a quick twist of his thumb and index finger. This... would require careful thought. He was trying to figure out why there were so many straps when Megan spoke.

"It's a sports bra."

"I knew that."

"Two-part—one part compresses, one part supports."

"Compresses?"

"Well, yeah. Otherwise, I'd be out to here." She gestured and Barry swallowed a whimper.

"You should never feel the need to compress."

"My shooting accuracy improves."

"And yet, you won't carry your gun."

She heard the disappointment in his voice and laughed. "What is it with you and my gun?"

"A certain image fueled by fantasy comic books."

"I don't look like those women!"

"I know. You don't have your gun."

Tugging down a strap, she laughed. "I *will* make you forget about that gun."

"Wait." He touched her shoulder. "Let me undress you. It's something I've been thinking about."

"You have?"

"Oh, yes." Barry checked once more to verify that there was no opening in the front and leaned forward so he could release her bra from behind. His fingers skimmed over the smooth skin of her back.

"Have you been thinking about undressing me just tonight, or before?"

"Before," he answered absently. Where were the hooks? The longer he searched, the more cool points he lost.

"How long before?"

Since about two seconds after the first time he'd seen her, but instead of telling her, he kissed her, running both hands over her back. The kiss was to allow him to discreetly figure out how to get the thing off her, but he forgot what he was doing and lost himself in the heat of her mouth.

Then she moaned and clutched at him and he never wanted to be found again. The taste of her, the feel of her lips, the texture of her skin, her touch…he wanted to separate all the sensations so he could fully appreciate them, but ultimately gave up and just focused on the pleasure.

Her tongue touched his and desire blotted out all conscious thought, not that he had much left, anyway.

Megan lifted her head, her hair falling forward and caressing either side of his face. He was about to tell her how sexy that was in case she didn't know when she said, "So how's that fantasy coming along?"

"This is better than any fantasy." He tunneled his fingers through her hair and recaptured the kiss, sucking on her lower lip.

"Mmm." She leaned insistently against him until they were prone on the couch.

One last time, Barry ran his hands up and down her back and over her shoulders, his fingers dancing along the straps.

And then he forgot all about the thing she'd swaddled herself in because Megan was aggressively exploring his mouth, taking the lead at a point he usually did.

Barry had a first-time sex pattern—a template of enjoyable moves that usually pleased his partner in an order guaranteed to bring results.

Megan broke his template and they were way out of order here. He was flying blind and didn't know what would happen next. The uncertainty made being with Megan all the more exciting and fresh and new and wonderful and erotic and hot and sexy and—*holy schomoley*. "No hands below the waist or we'll have a grand finale before we get the opening act."

She blinked innocently. "I'm just trying to take your jeans off."

"The snap is up *here*."

"I know, but I have my own fantasies."

He was all for equal-opportunity fantasies, but then she sat up and wiggled against him as she caressed her breasts.

Barry gasped. "For the love of—Megan!"

"You said no hands *below* the waist."

Even wearing that *thing*, she looked incredible and he could only imagine if she weren't wearing that thing and his imagination was getting him into serious trouble here. Clamping his eyes shut, Barry summoned Congressman Galloway's image to slow things down. When it didn't work, he mentally dressed him in women's clothing. That seemed to have the dampening effect he was going for.

"That's weird."

"What?" Nothing should be weird at this point.

Megan's brows drew together. "Earlier, when we were tied together, I could have sworn that…" She gave him a patently false smile. "Well, no matter. It's not what you've got, it's what you do with it."

What? "Hey! I've got it and I know what to do with it and when to do it."

She shrugged. "I'll give you two out of three."

Affronted, Barry didn't ask which two. "You must not be used to guys with finesse."

She grinned. "Oh, is that what you call it now?"

"You are *so* asking for it."

"I know. And I was hoping I wouldn't have to."

He just stopped himself from spluttering. "Come here." He reached for her, fingers once more searching for the secret entrance to the white fortress.

She bit her lip. He hoped it was in anticipation. He slipped his fingers beneath the back strap to the underneath layer, hoping he'd find some sort of hook, release it, and the whole thing would unravel. He was getting that thing off her if it killed him, and it just might.

"Barry." She straddled him again. "I know you've got your undressing fantasy, but it's just not working for me. How about you take off my jeans and I'll just…"

With a lightning movement, she tugged the hem on one side with both hands, and then pulled the whole thing off over her head sideways.

"I was going to try that next," Barry said. And then she turned back to him after tossing the unsexiest woman's undergarment he'd ever encountered over the back of the couch and he saw everything in slow motion.

Lush breasts sprang free, ringed by angry red elastic marks. She stopped moving before they did. There was a sexy bounce, then a sensual quiver, and finally a teasing ripple into stillness.

Barry felt his jaw drop. He hoped he wasn't drooling.

"My brothers subscribed to those comic books, so I'll try a pose for you. Promise me you'll massage my back if it goes out."

"I promise," he vowed fervently.

"Okay, here goes. Imagine an alien." She shook her hair with her fingers until it was appropriately tousled, assumed a fierce expression and arched her back, arm back as if holding a spear.

She was a warrior Amazon come to life. Every comic-book illustration he'd ever drooled over. Every fantasy his geeky self imagined. And a heck of a lot more fun than anyone he'd ever been with.

She was a keeper. The blood pounded in his temples and her image was permanently inducted into his Unforgettable Memories Hall of Fame. "You are a goddess. I am totally and completely unworthy."

"I dunno." Straightening her back, the goddess eyed him speculatively, swung her leg over him and stood. "Let's see what kind of finesse you're packing in those jeans."

She deserved a lot of finesse. Barry abandoned any hope of demonstrating his vaunted savoir faire and went for plain ole cool. But she'd made his knees weak and he stumbled as he stood, so Barry ended up just hoping he didn't fall down as he ripped at his zipper. He could be in serious trouble when he attempted to get his feet out of the jeans legs. He pulled at his briefs and jeans in one motion. *Concentrate. One leg at a time.* It was the little things that tripped a person up.

Barry was so focused on getting his jeans off without ending up flat on his backside that he failed to note Megan's expression.

"Okay." Her voice sounded strained. She cleared her throat. "Now I know why you weren't impressed by Dawn, the blow-up doll."

10

BARRY MADE HER FEEL feminine. Feminine not in the way Megan had thought she wanted—the way she suspected other women felt—but feminine in her own way. For the first time, she felt comfortable in her own skin.

She wasn't stupid. She knew men liked her breasts, but that had never made her feel particularly feminine. Honestly, a lot of the time, she felt her dates were dating them, not *her*.

Oh, Barry liked them, all right, but he liked her, too, which was a good thing, since she was totally besotted with him. And he'd quickly figure it out, if he hadn't already.

Megan's goal had changed. Her last Barry aversion therapy card had been written not flippantly, but seriously. If nothing else worked, she'd give in to her attraction for him and either get it out of her system—her original goal for this evening—or see where it led—her new goal.

Instead of making her inhibited because so much more was at stake, it freed her, and gave her a sexual confidence she seldom felt.

And wasn't it lucky that he had such a nice body?

"You're staring," he said.

"I'm liking." Megan let her gaze drift upward. "I'm liking a lot."

She stepped forward, brushed her breasts against his chest and watched his gaze heat. Maybe that had been her problem. She'd never really used them pro-actively before.

"You know," he began conversationally, "things are about to shift into a higher gear."

She had to admit he removed her jeans both effi-ciently and sensually. She also noted that there was a different gleam in his eye. Intent.

That gleam made her warm all over, but his mouth, now fused to hers, oh, his mouth made her hot.

She felt him stoop, their lips still locked, and then tightened her arms around his neck when his hand pressed against the backs of her knees. Seconds later, she was flat on her back on the couch and Barry's body covered hers.

"Nice move," she said.

"Nice *everything*," he murmured. He laughed softly. "Words are my life, but that's the best I can come up with."

As he spoke, he caressed the length of her body, and her nerve endings went wild.

"So keep talking with your hands." She liked his hands. She was having a perfectly lovely conversa-tion with his hands, especially when they got around to talking to her breasts.

Showing remarkable restraint, Barry had sensi-tized the skin all around with light, feathery touches, taking his time until Megan thought she was going to have to shove her chest at him. When he finally lavished the attention she'd craved, a guttural moan escaped her. She simply did not make sounds like that—not involuntary ones, anyway.

But Barry had made her wait and wait and then it was really worth the wait and then she needed more.

He no doubt needed something, too, but Megan had been so caught up in her own pleasure, she'd forgotten about him.

He was going to think she was an awful lover.

"Bar-ry," she gasped. "I—need—"

"I know what you need." His voice was as guttural as her moan. "I need it, too."

She'd meant that she needed to reciprocate and quit being so greedy, but he started doing very interesting things with his fingers and she, well, forgot.

Barry leaned to the side and Megan took the opportunity to run her hands over his chest, down his sides, over his flanks and everywhere she could reach. This wasn't a time to be particular and the little tingles she got when she touched him were kinda cool.

Barry straightened and smiled down at her. He was clearly ready. And while that was great, frankly, Megan thought she might have some ground to make up, but Barry slid his body up hers and began to work magic with that mouth of his and it was truly amazing how fast he took her from *Well, okay*, to *Hurry up before I explode*.

Then Barry rocked inside of her and she did explode, faster and harder than she ever had before. The surprise was almost as much fun as the ride. And Barry, holding her while still moving, nuzzling the side of her neck and murmuring who-knew-what was just so…so delicious.

He was better at this than she'd expected. The great technique, she'd figured was a given. The emotional intimacy, she hadn't. It was definitely the kind of thing that made a girl come back for more.

She was enjoying the float back down when Barry tensed, muttered something that sounded suspiciously like, "I love you," and shuddered with his own release.

But it couldn't be. And even if he had said he loved her, she knew better than to hold a man responsible for what he said during the heat of passion.

But that didn't mean she couldn't believe it for the next few moments. So Megan wrapped her arms around Barry, whose head was pillowed against her chest, and believed.

"You are really good at this," she told him. "Next round is on me."

THE NEXT ROUND was definitely on her, not that she was complaining and she made sure Barry had no complaints, either, if she did say so herself. Incoherent babbling wasn't complaining, was it? She was proud that she'd reduced him to incoherent babbling. And she liked that I'll-do-anything-for-you expression in his eyes.

Afterward, he pulled her to him so her back was nestled against his chest. Raising her hair, he blew against the dampness at her nape. "Hot, sweaty sex. Just what you ordered."

And he'd wanted to make love, she remembered,

biting her lip. How ironic that she'd made love and he'd had the hot, sweaty sex.

"This has been the best night of my life," he said quietly into the darkness.

If she answered, he'd know she loved him; he'd hear it in her voice. And nothing made a man run quicker than realizing a woman was thinking love when all he was thinking was sex.

So she said nothing and after a while, her eyelids grew heavy and she knew that they'd better move soon, or she'd fall asleep. "What time is it?"

"Hmm...I don't know—four? Five?"

"We'd better get going."

He tightened his arm around her. "Not yet. There's no place else I'd rather be."

And because she felt the same way, Megan sighed against him, savored the way his arms felt around her...and fell asleep.

VOICES. LIGHT. More voices.

Megan had a split second of disorientation before she realized what was happening. An arm tightened around her and Barry's soft curse reminded her of who it was happening with.

Omigoshomigoshomigosh she was naked on a couch in Congressman Galloway's campaign headquarters and people were about to come in.

"Barry!"

"Shh. We can salvage this. Get dressed."

"Oh, sure we can. Ow!" Megan gasped as she peeled herself off the couch. The leather grain was visible on her skin.

She grabbed her jeans and underwear first. She didn't dare look at him because hysterical giggles were just below the surface. Heck, plain old hysteria was just below the surface. She would have never *ever* believed she'd find herself in this situation. It was unreal.

"Are you sure we can't just go in?" said one of the voices.

No.

"Don't you watch TV? There's police tape. We gotta wait until they get here and tell us it's okay."

Megan exhaled and took back every criticism she'd leveled against cop shows.

"So, who wants to make a coffee run?"

Megan worked herself into her bra. "What are they doing here? It's Saturday!" she mouthed at Barry.

Barry had stopped moving and was staring at her, transfixed. Flattering, but not the time. She gestured toward his shirt as she found her own.

Maybe they could sneak out the back. Megan grabbed her shoes, crammed everything—she hoped—back into her purse, righted the pencil mug and gestured wildly for Barry to follow her.

He shook his head and looked at her.

"What?" It was a silent scream.

He walked over as he buttoned his shirt. "We act like we're supposed to be here," he whispered.

"You mean we act like we were *supposed* to break in and have sex on the couch? Oh, God, it's leather. It probably smells like sex. I wonder if there's Lysol in the bathroom?"

She whirled away from him and headed to the

tiny unisex bathroom and searched in the cabinet beneath the sink.

There was a can of Spring Mountain scent. She'd never felt such affection for air freshener before.

After dropping her purse and shoes, she took the can, ran back to the couch and sprayed. Barry grabbed her wrist.

"Too much is a giveaway." His gaze flicked to her hair and lingered a beat too long.

Running back to the bathroom, Megan saw herself in the mirror.

Disaster. All the gunk the salon had put in her hair had resculpted her hair, leaving it flat on one side and sticking out wildly on the other. It was the worst case of bed head—couch head—in hairstyling history.

She dampened her hair and tried to fluff up one side and flatten the other. The effort was marginally effective.

Barry stood watching her from the doorway. How could he be so calm? "Here." He handed her a rubber band and Megan gratefully scraped her hair back in its familiar style.

And then he kissed her.

Lovely, but…"We don't have time—"

"Everything is going to work out." He tucked one of her new shorter layers behind her ear. "Trust me."

It wasn't that Megan didn't trust him, it was that she wanted everything to work out without her dying of embarrassment.

"It's coffee!" A cheer went up from outside.

"That's our cue," Barry said.

"Cue? Cue for what?"

He turned off the light and pulled her out of the bathroom, correctly guessing that her first instinct was to lock herself inside. "Put your shoes by the couch."

"Why?"

"It'll look like we've been here awhile and don't have anything to hide."

Megan was just going to go with him on that one. He looked around.

"In the trash can," she reminded him.

"Right." He found his shoe, dropped it by the couch with the other, then cast a glance around the room before heading to the door.

"What are you doing?"

"Letting them in."

He was *what?* But Barry opened the door. He actually did it. He opened the door. "Well, good morning," he said and Megan felt her face flame hot enough to cook eggs.

Oh, good. Breakfast for everyone.

There was shocked silence from the group waiting outside. Megan understood. She was shocked, herself.

"Who are you? What are you doing here?" one of them asked. "You should know that we've called the police."

Barry casually gestured toward Megan. "The police are already here. And now, I want to know what you're doing here on a Saturday morning," he said in a school-principal voice.

A young woman responded. "Congressman Galloway sent us to clean up after the break-in and see what was taken. He'll be here in a half hour for a press conference."

"Hang on, Meredith." A younger guy took a long sip of coffee and nodded to Megan. "If she's police, then what are you?"

"Barry Sutton, *Dallas Press*." Thrusting out his hand, Barry gave him a sincere Barry-smile that Megan hoped worked. "I'm early for the press conference."

"Aren't you that reporter from last year?" Hostility radiated from the guy. "The one who caused so much trouble for Congressman Galloway?"

Barry widened his smile. "I'm baaaack."

Pushing past him, the coffee guy headed for Megan. "Let's see some ID."

Megan tried to be as nonchalant as Barry. And she was, until she couldn't find her badge in her purse. Quickly, she scanned the couch and the area around it, but the thing was gone. "I've misplaced—"

"Oh, sure. Have you got a gun? Show me that."

Megan shook her head, conscious of Barry's wince.

"Okay, nobody leaves, nobody moves." Coffee guy backed his way to the entrance and blocked it.

"She *is* a police officer," Barry reiterated.

Megan didn't feel like one at the moment.

"The police are here," someone said from outside.

Through the open door, Megan saw a cruiser park at the curb.

Okay, so her career was over. Right now, embarrassment was the least of her worries. Barry couldn't grasp the extent of the trouble they were in. Why hadn't he just escaped out the back with her?

She glanced toward Barry and he pointed to her

shoes, indicating that she should put them on. Well, it was something to do while the coffee guy gleefully tattled on them.

She'd finished tying her cross trainers when the two officers cautiously approached, weapons drawn.

They holstered them as soon as they saw her. "Hey, Esterbrook. What are you doing here?"

"Hey, O'Reilly, Sanchez." She nodded to them, feeling a brief satisfaction at the deflated expression on the coffee guy's face.

"Oh, no. It's Sutton." O'Reilly shook his head. "Okay, y'all. What's up?"

She knew Barry was getting ready to answer and she knew that nobody would believe whatever he said. "What's up? I'll tell you what's up," she said. And then she did something she'd never done in her life....

She lied.

HE REALLY WISHED she'd kept quiet, but she was doing a good job so far. Barry listened as Megan brought the patrolmen up to speed from last night and then went further.

"I thought I saw the suspect returning to the scene and remained on surveillance. Sutton had been monitoring police frequencies and arrived." She threw him a disgusted look that matched the ones Sanchez and O'Reilly had given him. She was pretty good at it.

"When the press refused to leave, I remained to secure the site."

"Inside?"

"I ascertained that it would be the only way to protect both the scene and the media present."

"Yeah." And the two men threw him another one of those looks, but they stopped questioning Megan.

They bought it! They actually bought it! He and Megan were home free. Not only that, he was first on the scene for a press conference.

The coffee guy—Jason, Barry had learned—was making a red-faced apology to Megan. Barry tried to give her a thumbs-up behind the kid's back, but stopped when he saw her miserable, guilty face.

He instantly knew what caused her expression. She'd lied, and with an insight he didn't particularly welcome, Barry knew that if Megan's lie was allowed to stand, it would eat away at her.

Well, there was nothing for it. He was going to have to tell the truth.

He waited until Jason had left, and Sanchez and O'Reilly were talking to Megan before he approached her and flung an arm around her shoulders.

She shrugged it off, her body stiff.

"I'm not real clear why you happened on the scene and then wouldn't leave, Sutton."

Barry gave Sanchez an aw-shucks grin. "Looking for a story."

"At 3:00 a.m.?"

O'Reilly spoke. "Come to think of it, Esterbrook, *you* being here at 3:00 a.m. is—"

"Megan, honey—" Barry broke in.

She threw him a horrified don't-honey-me look.

"We're going to have to tell them." And then he continued talking in spite of the elbow she dug into his ribs. "Guys, well, the truth is Megan and I broke in here so we could have hot, sweaty sex on the congressman's couch."

Megan's face went white, red and then white again. At that moment, Barry figured she hated him, but he also figured it wouldn't last. If she would just *trust* him.

Everybody looked at the couch in question. Then O'Reilly smirked. "So, uh, Megan. You confirm that?"

Megan glared betrayal at Barry, who smiled at her. "Megan, I sincerely want you to confirm that."

She blinked.

He added the other half of her smile, and then deliberately winked.

"You—" She looked at Sanchez and O'Reilly. "Okay. Yeah. I broke crime-scene tape and picked the lock just so I could spend the night having hot, and, was it sweaty sex?"

Barry nodded.

"Right. Hot and sweaty sex with Barry Sutton. Yeah. That's what we did. All night. Three, maybe four times. I lost count."

There was silence and then the two officers began howling with laughter. "You and Sutton. That's a good one!"

"Hey, man," Sanchez said to him. "Knowing how she feels about you, take my advice and don't let her within ten feet of your—"

"He's here! Galloway's here!"

The congressman's staff rushed outside, followed by O'Reilly and Sanchez.

Megan turned to Barry. Her color had improved, he noticed.

"How could you—"

"Tell the truth? And to think you lied. I am shocked, Ms. Esterbrook, utterly shocked."

She opened her mouth, closed it, fighting a smile. "Barry—"

He put his hands on her shoulders, his face serious. "I told you, when you're lying, it's always best to tell the truth. You're not responsible if they don't believe you." He dropped his hands. "I'd kiss you now, but I don't want to spoil the story in case they're watching."

"You are *so* lucky that it worked." She bent down and looked under the couch.

"There was no luck involved. Only skill. Find your badge?"

"It's under here." She moved the couch and reached beneath it. "I should be mad."

"Why?" Watching her on her hands and knees reminded Barry of some of the enjoyable moments they'd had on that very couch. He should offer to buy that couch.

"Anger seems like the correct response."

"But you're not angry?"

"No." She stood and patted the couch. "Kinda turned on, actually."

"That's my girl."

Galloway entered the room, all bluster and political savvy.

"Ah." Barry grinned at her. "Now, we get our jobs back. Follow my lead."

"Absolutely, oh skilled one."

"Congressman!" Barry called.

Startled recognition crossed Galloway's face an instant before the political mask slipped back into place. "I'll talk to the press briefly at ten-thirty, after which I'm due to attend the wedding of the daughter of an old friend."

"I know. I'll be there, too. I just thought you'd like to talk to me now." Barry glanced at the hovering staff. "In private." And then he leveled a long look at Galloway.

Donald Galloway was too seasoned not to understand the significance of that kind of look and the importance of early damage control. "We can go into my office, unless...?"

"We don't think the intruder had time to get into your office, but your staff hasn't yet had the opportunity to verify that nothing has been disturbed," Megan told him.

"And I think we'll do better out back," Barry said. "Visual aids, you know."

After a few words to Jason, Galloway joined them by Megan's car. Out of sight of his staff, he dropped his avuncular expression and looked exactly like what he was—a powerful man who'd been cornered.

Barry knew better than to waste time. "Last year I wrote an article."

"Which ruined an investigation in which I was involved."

Barry nodded. "As a result, I was banished to the land of hearts and flowers and Megan, here, lost her job as police spokeswoman. I think you had something to do with that."

"Yours, but not hers," Galloway conceded after a moment.

"Either way, we want our jobs back." It was time to lay their cards on the table. "Megan, go ahead and open the trunk. Here's what we know—you don't have a sister. You're a cross-dresser and you're being blackmailed."

Galloway stared, stone-faced.

Barry hadn't expected an instant confession. "Don't worry. I've recently been persuaded that sometimes, one has to sacrifice for the greater good." Barry smiled at Megan.

"I don't understand," Galloway said.

"That should worry me," Barry said to him. "But come here."

They looked in the trunk where a deflated Dawn gazed limply back at them.

Galloway's upper lip beaded with sweat.

"This was what was placed in your office last night," Barry continued. "Megan and I have gone out on a limb here. We're the only ones who know about this—but don't get any ideas. I scheduled an explanatory text message that'll go out to the wire services if I don't cancel it."

"In the event of an unfortunate accident? You've been watching too many movies." Galloway gave him a wintry smile. "So you know." He met Barry's eyes and Barry had to give the man credit for that. "What's it going to cost me?"

"Nothing," Megan said.

"You are not a good negotiator," Barry told her.

"We are going to report this evidence, but only to

those who already know about your…you," Megan said. "We know there's more to this situation…there is, isn't there?"

Galloway exhaled heavily and looked at Barry.

"I'm not writing about the doll or your cross-dressing," Barry assured him. "In return, I want an exclusive when you can give me one."

"That seems equitable."

"Yeah, well, Megan's been a bad influence on me."

"Hey," she said without heat.

Galloway gave them an assessing look and then abruptly began speaking. "A couple of years ago, in the interest of national security, I allowed myself to appear vulnerable to bribery and blackmail. We had some nibbles when you broke the story. Unfortunately, after that I was no longer of use to the investigation. However, certain angry parties who'd been snared in the net discovered my harmless secret and began blackmailing me in earnest."

"And by chance are a certain groom and best man involved in dealing with the blackmailer?"

Galloway gazed at Barry. "Recent developments indicate that I'm not the only one in my situation and that's all I can tell you."

"At least tell me if there's going to be a wedding."

"I plan to be at St. Andrew's at eleven-thirty," the congressman answered him stonily.

They stared at each other. "You don't know if the wedding's on or not, do you? Which means Gus hasn't shown up at the church yet."

Galloway was silent.

"Oh, come on. I can't miss out on *two* stories."

They took each other's measure and Barry saw all hostility leave the congressman's face.

"I can't help you with the wedding, but I give you my word that when I can, I will tell you the entire story concerning the other matter. Who knows? You could get a book out of it." Galloway offered Barry his hand and Barry, trying not to break out into a victory dance, shook it.

His elation lasted for all of two seconds. "Can you do anything for Megan? Maybe put in a good word?"

Galloway shook his head and turned to her. "You're tainted."

Megan gasped. "But...I didn't do anything wrong!"

"It doesn't matter. It's all perception. You will never get your job back, or if you do, it will be years and it won't be with the Dallas police."

She looked crushed and it broke Barry's heart. "Aw, Megan." She looked up at him and he knew she wanted him to tell her that the congressman was wrong. "Galloway's right."

She slumped against her car.

"However," Galloway continued, "I'd like to offer you a job on my staff as a media liaison. Even without knowing your current salary, I can guarantee your new one would be at least double."

"I don't need your charity," she snapped.

"Hmm. Much as this goes against my own best interest, I must point out that you're pure gold. You are a trained police officer with extensive large-market media experience. You're licensed to carry a gun and you know how to use it. You're familiar with security procedures and you can think on your feet. You'll be aware of potential problems while you're dealing with crowds and the press." He smiled wryly. "Also, you're aware of my little secret. So now that you know how uniquely valuable you are, you can get a job with any of my political colleagues or foes."

"Probably for more money," Barry pointed out.

"However," Galloway continued after a glance at Barry, "adjusting to the political environment takes time and you'll make mistakes. Should you accept my offer, you'll find that I will be, up to a point, very forgiving of those mistakes. Others will not be. Interested?"

Wow. Barry hadn't expected Galloway to offer Megan a job, but it made absolutely perfect sense. He reluctantly raised his opinion of the man a notch. Okay, a couple of notches, since before he was convinced the guy was a crook and now he figured he was just unlucky.

Megan stared at Galloway. "That was quite a speech."

Why wasn't she jumping on the opportunity? Barry nudged her. "Thank the nice man, Megan."

"Why?"

He wanted to shake her. "It's perfect for you! You're such a political rah-rah. You'll love it."

"I don't know." She continued to study Galloway. "You're honest, aren't you?" she asked him flat out. "Because I don't lie—at least…" She flushed.

"She doesn't lie," Barry confirmed. "She's really bad at it. No experience. Her face turns red, too."

A red-faced Megan ignored him. "I'm not going to work for something or somebody I don't believe in."

"Fair enough." Galloway cleared his throat. "To answer your question, I do my best for my constituents given the realities of political life."

A typical political nonanswer. Straight-arrow Megan would never go for it, Barry thought.

But she did. Smiling, she said, "If you'd told me you were completely honest, I wouldn't have believed you. Intelligently honest, I can handle. Trying to do your best, I can handle. Making honest mistakes—okay. But if I work for you and I find out you're a crook—I'm calling him." She stuck her thumb at Barry.

"What's intelligently honest?" Barry wanted this clarified. "Honest is honest."

"Intelligently honest is keeping Dawn in the trunk until she meets the right people." Megan slammed the trunk lid closed.

"Wow." Barry looked at the congressman. "You might not be able to afford her."

"Does this mean you're going to be working for me?" Galloway asked.

"In D.C. and Dallas?" Megan asked him.

"A lot of time in D.C. More than in Dallas. You'd have to relocate. However, if I recall, Meredith, a woman on my staff—you may have encountered her this morning—is looking for a roommate, if that'll sway you. Perhaps you could stay with her until you get your bearings."

Megan gave Barry a look he couldn't interpret. Was she looking for reassurance? "It's a great opportunity for you," he told her.

Still she hesitated. "I'll consider it," she told Galloway. "In the meantime, you've got a press conference scheduled. Mind if I have a trial run?"

Congressman Galloway smiled, looking relaxed for the first time in a long while. "Excellent idea."

MEGAN WAS BACK in her element. It was uncanny. She didn't know the congressman, but she knew exactly how to tell the story of the break-ins to the press, giving them a little information so they'd stop digging for the bigger, hidden prize.

Barry was one who never stopped digging.

Except this time. He dutifully positioned himself in the pack of reporters and didn't make faces at her or ask her awkward questions—and she missed it.

"You were too easy on me," she told him afterward.

He looked pained. "I already knew all the answers. You do realize I'm sitting on the biggest story of my life."

"And showing fabulous restraint."

"Speaking of restraint...wanna come back here when everybody is gone?"

It wouldn't be the same, Megan knew. "Don't you have a wedding to cover?"

"Yes. Yes, I do." He sounded so full of regret that she laughed.

"But now that you know what Gus and Derek were doing—"

"But I don't know *exactly* what they were doing and that's what's killing me."

"But you will. And what if Gus didn't make it back to the wedding? That could be some kinda story."

He grinned. "I'm finding renewed enthusiasm for this wedding. Wanna come?"

Megan felt funny about going to a wedding to which she hadn't been invited, never mind that she was dressed completely inappropriately. She let Barry drive her car while she tried to fix her hair and repair her makeup. The ponytail was going to have to stay and removing the smudges under her eyes was about the best she could do, since she didn't have any makeup with her.

"You should have told me I had raccoon eyes before I did the press conference."

"It gave you credibility. You looked like you'd been up all night dealing with a crisis."

Which brought to mind exactly what they *had* been doing for a huge chunk of the night—early morning. It also brought to mind what they *hadn't* said.

Specifically, Barry had said nothing except urged her to take a job that would require her to live in Washington, D.C. for most of the year.

She supposed that was her answer.

He parked her car beside a silver florist's van and they walked around to the front of the church.

Megan couldn't stand it. She couldn't watch another woman get married when she wanted...

"I'm going to take the job with the congressman," she announced just as they reached the bottom of the church steps.

"I think it's a good move," he said quietly, and then looked away.

She waited for him to say more. Anything more. *Ask me to stay, damn it.*

"I guess that's it, then," were his words.

That was *not* what she wanted him to say.

"I…I won't be in D.C. all the time…" She heard the pleading in her voice and told herself to stop it.

"Yeah."

They started to climb the steps.

"I can't do this." Barry stopped and turned to her. "There's a rule or something that says you can't take a woman to a wedding without knowing how she feels about you."

How could he not know? "I have never heard this rule."

"I've been to more weddings than you have." He swallowed. "The thing is, twice I've told you that I love you and you, well, haven't said anything back."

Megan's mouth dropped open. "You told me during—" She looked all around them. "During *sex!* Everybody knows when a man tells you he loves you during sex it doesn't count!"

"It counts!"

"Yeah, well, he only means it right then, not the next day."

"This is still the same day. Besides, I told you once before."

"When? Oh. Because I was doing something you wanted. You didn't mean that, either."

Barry looked appealingly frustrated. "I have never had a conversation like this before. So when does it count? On the steps of a church?" He gestured to the gray marble. "Is this good enough? I love you, Megan."

She *wanted* to believe him, but…"Since when?"

Barry looked heavenward. "Why am I having such trouble here? Okay, I think there was always something going on between us, but I didn't know what it was until Elvis told me. You know, when we danced. Like the song said, I couldn't help falling in love with you." He reached for her.

"Oh." Something shifted in her heart. "Elvis." Elvis had suddenly become her favorite singer. "The diner." *Their* restaurant. Tears formed in her eyes and spilled down her cheeks. "You gave me your friiiiii-eeeessss," she wailed and then she gave a great sniff.

Barry drew her to him. "And women wonder why guys don't like to say the *L* word."

He loved her. Barry Sutton loved her. Slowly, Megan allowed herself to believe. "You're serious?"

"Good God, woman, we're in full view of a church. A man is always serious then. If that's not already a rule, it should be."

She flung her arms around him. "I fell for you when you held my hand in the parking lot."

"Huh?"

"You told me you wanted to get to know me better and wanted me to know you and then you held my hand." She sniffed again. "And you went through all the cards and you...well, you're just you."

"And that's why I love you." He kissed her on her forehead.

Megan sighed happily against him. "I'll tell the congressman I won't take the job."

"Oh, you are *so* taking that job. Listen, you know I've been wanting to get back into crime reporting—what better place than the Washington political scene? And won't you just love having a familiar face in the crowd?"

"Barry!"

He laughed and held her hand as the sounds of a string quartet floated out from the church.

"That sounds like wedding music," Megan said. "Do you think that's a good sign?"

Barry looked at his watch. "It's eleven-thirty. Right on time. Let's go see if Derek and Gus made it back. Oh, and by the way—I promise not to be late for *our* wedding."

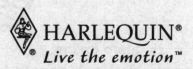

HARLEQUIN®

Temptation.

One frantic bride, one missing groom
and twenty-four hours for three
couples to discover they're meant
to live happily ever after....

24 Hours: The Wedding

Don't miss these fabulous stories by three of
Temptation's favorite authors!

FALLING FOR YOU by Heather MacAllister
Harlequin Temptation #1014
March 2005

KISS AND RUN by Barbara Daly
Harlequin Temptation #1018
April 2005

ONE NIGHT IN TEXAS by Jane Sullivan
Harlequin Temptation #1022
May 2005

On sale this spring at your favorite retail outlet.

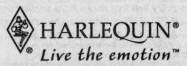

HARLEQUIN®
Live the emotion™

www.eHarlequin.com   HT24W

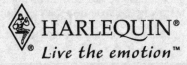

presents:

New York Times
bestselling author

JOAN HOHL

A MAN APART

(SD #1640, available
March 2005)

The moment rancher Justin Grainger laid eyes on
sexy Hannah Deturk, he vowed not to leave town
without getting into her bed. Their whirlwind affair left
them both wanting more. But Hannah feared falling
for a loner like Justin could only mean heartache...
unless she convinced him to be a man apart no longer.

Available at your favorite retail outlet.

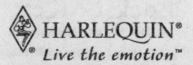